TEDIOUS BRIEF TALES OF GRANTA AND GRAMARYE

BY INGULPHUS
[ARTHUR GRAY]

OLEANDER PRESS

The Oleander Press
16 Orchard Street
Cambridge
CB1 1JT

www.oleanderpress.com

First published by W. Heffer & Sons: 1919
This edition published by The Oleander Press: 2009

This edition © 2009. All rights reserved.

No part of this publication may be reproduced, stored in a retrieval system, or transmitted, in any form or by any means without the prior permission in writing of the publisher, nor be otherwise circulated in any form of binding or cover other than in which it is published and without a similar condition including this condition being imposed on the subsequent purchaser.

A CIP catalogue record for the book is
available from the British Library.

ISBN: 9780906672860

Designed and typeset by Hamish Symington
www.hamishsymington.com

Printed in England

Entrance Gateway,
Jesus College.

First published December 1919

These tales originally appeared in *The Cambridge Review*, *The Gownsman* and *Chanticlere* (the Jesus College Magazine).

Tedious Brief Tales of Granta and Gramarye

by

"Ingulphus"
(Arthur Gray, Master of Jesus College)

with illustrations by
E. Joyce Shillington Scales

"Merry and tragical, tedious and brief:
That is hot ice and wondrous strange snow."
A Midsummer Night's Dream

Contents

The Everlasting Club	1
The Treasure of John Badcoke	13
The True History of Anthony Ffryar	27
The Necromancer	39
Brother John's Bequest	51
The Burden of Dead Books	67
Thankfull Thomas	93
The Palladium	107
The Sacrist of Saint Radegund	119

List of Illustrations

Entrance Gateway, Jesus College	Frontispiece
Doorway, Cow Lane	6
Oriel Window of Hall and Entrance to "K" Staircase	15
Old Hall, Master's Lodge	23
North-West Corner of Cloisters	28
The Master's Stall	33
Main Gateway and Porter's Lodge	42
On "O" Staircase	45
Fireplace in Master's Lodge	57
A Corner of the Library	69
Chapel Doorway in Master's Garden	79
Norman Gallery, North Transept	98
South-West Pier of Tower	103
In the Fens	117
Entrance to Chapter House	124
The Chancel Squint	127

To Two Cambridge Magicians

In London lanes, uncanonized, untold
By letter'd brass or stone, apart they lie,
Dead and unreck'd of by the passer-by.
Here still they seem together, as of old,
To breathe our air, to walk our Cambridge ground,
Here still to after learners to impart
Hints of the magic that gave Faustus art
To make blind Homer sing "with ravishing sound
To his melodious harp" of Oenon, dead
For Alexander's love; that framed the spell
Of him who, in the Friar's "secret cell,"
Made the great marvel of the Brazen Head.
Marlowe and Greene, on you a Cambridge hand
Sprinkles these pious particles of sand.

The Everlasting Club

HERE IS A chamber in Jesus College the existence of which is probably known to few who are now resident, and fewer still have penetrated into it or even seen its interior. It is on the right hand of the landing on the top floor of the precipitous staircase in the angle of the cloister next the Hall – a staircase which, for some forgotten story connected with it, is traditionally called 'Cow Lane'. The padlock which secures its massive oaken door is very rarely unfastened, for the room is bare and unfurnished. Once it served as a place of deposit for superfluous kitchen ware, but even that ignominious use has passed from it, and it is now left to undisturbed solitude and darkness. For I should say that it is entirely cut off from the light of

the outer day by the walling up, some time in the eighteenth century, of its single window, and such light as ever reaches it comes from the door, when rare occasion causes it to be opened.

Yet at no extraordinarily remote day this chamber has evidently been tenanted, and, before it was given up to darkness, was comfortably fitted, according to the standard of comfort which was known in college in the days of George II. There is still a roomy fireplace before which legs have been stretched and wine and gossip have circulated in the days of wigs and brocade. For the room is spacious and, when it was lighted by the window looking eastward over the fields and common, it must have been a cheerful place for a sociable don.

Let me state in brief, prosaic outline the circumstances which account for the gloom and solitude in which this room has remained now for nearly a century and a half.

In the second quarter of the eighteenth century the University possessed a great variety of clubs of a social kind. There were clubs in college parlours and clubs in private rooms, or in inns and coffee-houses: clubs flavoured with politics, clubs clerical, clubs purporting to be learned and literary. Whatever their professed particularity, the aim of each was convivial. Some of them, which included undergraduates as well as seniors, were dissipated enough, and in their limited provincial way aped the profligacy of such clubs as the Hell Fire Club of London notoriety.

Among these last was one which was at once more select and of more evil fame than any of its fellows. By a singular accident, presently to be explained, the Minute Book of this Club, including the years from 1738 to 1766, came into the hands of a Master of Jesus College, and though, so far as I am aware, it is no longer extant, I have before me a transcript of it which, though it is in a recent handwriting, presents in a bald shape such a singular array of facts that I must ask you to accept them as veracious. The original book is described as a stout duodecimo volume bound in red leather and fastened with red silken strings. The writing in it occupied some 40 pages, and ended with the date November 2, 1766.

The Club in question was called the Everlasting Club – a name sufficiently explained by its rules, set forth in the pocket-book. Its number was limited to seven, and it would seem that its members were all young men, between 22 and 30. One of them was a Fellow-Commoner of Trinity: three of them were Fellows of Colleges, among whom I should specially mention a Fellow of Jesus, named Charles Bellasis: another was a landed proprietor in the county, and the sixth was a young Cambridge physician. The Founder and President of the Club was the Honourable Alan Dermot, who, as the son of an Irish Peer, had obtained a nobleman's degree in the University, and lived in idleness in the town. Very little is known of his life and character, but that little is highly in his disfavour. He was killed in a duel in Paris in the year 1743, under circumstances which I need not particularise, but which point to an exceptional degree of cruelty and wickedness in the slain man.

I will quote from the first pages of the Minute Book some of the laws of the Club, which will explain its constitution:–

1. "This Society consisteth of seven Everlastings, who may be Corporeal or Incorporeal, as Destiny shall determine.
2. The rules of the Society, as herein written, are immutable and Everlasting.
3. None shall hereafter be chosen into the Society and none shall cease to be members.
4. The Honourable Alan Dermot is the Everlasting President of the Society.
5. The Senior Corporeal Everlasting, not being the President, shall be the Secretary of the Society, and in this Book of Minutes shall record its transactions, the date at which any Everlasting shall cease to be Corporeal, and all fines due to the Society. And when such Senior Everlasting shall cease to be Corporeal he shall, either in person or by some sure hand, deliver this Book of Minutes to him who shall be next Senior and at the time Corporeal, and he shall in like manner record the transactions therein and transmit it to the next Senior. The neglect of these provisions shall be visited by the President with fine or punishment according to his discretion.
6. On the second day of November in every year, being the Feast of All Souls, at ten o'clock *post meridiem*, the Everlastings shall meet at supper in the place of residence of that Corporeal member of the Society to whom it shall fall in order of rotation to entertain them, and they shall all subscribe in this Book of Minutes their names and present place of abode.

7. It shall be the obligation of every Everlasting to be present at the yearly entertainment of the Society, and none shall allege for excuse that he has not been invited thereto. If any Everlasting shall fail to attend the yearly meeting, or in his turn shall fail to provide entertainment for the Society, he shall be mulcted at the discretion of the President.

8. Nevertheless, if in any year, in the month of October, and not less than seven days before the Feast of All Souls, the major part of the Society, that is to say, four at the least, shall meet and record in writing in these Minutes that it is their desire that no entertainment be given in that year, then, notwithstanding the two rules last rehearsed, there shall be no entertainment in that year, and no Everlasting shall be mulcted on the ground of his absence."

The rest of the rules are either too profane or too puerile to be quoted here. They indicate the extraordinary levity with which the members entered on their preposterous obligations. In particular, to the omission of any regulation as to the transmission of the Minute Book after the last Everlasting ceased to be "Corporeal," we owe the accident that it fell into the hands of one who was not a member of the society, and the consequent preservation of its contents to the present day.

Low as was the standard of morals in all classes of the University in the first half of the eighteenth century, the flagrant defiance of public decorum by the members of the Everlasting Society brought

Doorway, Cow Lane.

upon it the stern censure of the authorities, and after a few years it was practically dissolved and its members banished from the University. Charles Bellasis, for instance, was obliged to leave the college, and, though he retained his fellowship, he remained absent from it for nearly twenty years. But the minutes of the society reveal a more terrible reason for its virtual extinction.

Between the years 1738 and 1743 the minutes record many meetings of the Club, for it met on other occasions besides that of All Souls Day. Apart from a great deal of impious jocularity on the part of the writers, they are limited to the formal record of the attendance of the members, fines inflicted, and so forth. The meeting on November 2nd in the latter year is the first about which there is any departure from the stereotyped forms. The supper was given in the house of the physician. One member, Henry Davenport, the former Fellow-Commoner of Trinity, was absent from the entertainment, as he was then serving in Germany, in the Dettingen campaign. The minutes contain an entry, "Mulctatus propter absentiam per Presidentem, Hen. Davenport." An entry on the next page of the book runs, "Henry Davenport by a Cannon-shot became an Incorporeal Member, November 3, 1743."

The minutes give in their own handwriting, under date November 2, the names and addresses of the six other members. First in the list, in a large bold hand, is the autograph of "Alan Dermot, President, at the Court of His Royal Highness." Now in October Dermot had certainly been in attendance on the Young Pretender at Paris, and doubtless the address which he gave was understood at the time by the other Everlastings to refer to the fact. But on October 28, five days *before* the meeting of the Club, he was killed, as I have already mentioned, in a duel. The news of his death cannot have reached Cambridge on November 2, for the Secretary's record of it is placed below that of Davenport, and with the date November 10: "this day was reported that the President was become an Incorporeal by the hands of a French chevalier." And in a sudden ebullition, which is in glaring contrast with his previous profanities, he has dashed down "The Good God shield us from ill."

The tidings of the President's death scattered the Everlastings like a thunderbolt. They left Cambridge and buried themselves in widely parted regions. But the Club did not cease to exist. The Secretary was still bound to his hateful records: the five survivors did not dare to neglect their fatal obligations. Horror of the presence of the President made the November gathering once and for ever impossible: but horror, too, forbade them to neglect the precaution of meeting in October of every year to put in writing their objection to the celebration. For five years five names are appended to that entry in the minutes, and that is all the business of the Club. Then another member died, who was not the Secretary.

For eighteen more years four miserable men met once each year to deliver the same formal protest. During those years we gather from the signatures that Charles Bellasis returned to Cambridge, now, to appearance, chastened and decorous. He occupied the rooms which I have described on the staircase in the corner of the cloister.

Then in 1766 comes a new handwriting and an altered minute:

"Jan. 27, on this day Francis Witherington, Secretary, became an Incorporeal Member. The same day this Book was delivered to me, James Harvey." Harvey lived only a month, and a similar entry on March 7 states that the book has descended, with the same mysterious celerity, to William Catherston. Then, on May 18, Charles Bellasis writes that on that day, being the date of Catherston's decease, the Minute Book has come to him as the last surviving Corporeal of the Club.

As it is my purpose to record fact only I shall not attempt to describe the feelings of the unhappy Secretary when he penned that fatal record. When Witherington died it must have come home to the three survivors that after twenty-three years' intermission the ghastly entertainment must be annually renewed, with the addition of fresh incorporeal guests, or that they must undergo the pitiless censure of the President. I think it likely that the terror of the alternative, coupled with the mysterious delivery of the Minute Book, was answerable for the speedy decease of the two first successors to the Secretaryship. Now that the alternative was offered to Bellasis alone, he was firmly resolved to bear the consequences, whatever they might be, of an infringement of the Club rules.

The graceless days of George II had passed away from the University. They were succeeded by times of outward respectability, when religion and morals were no longer publicly challenged. With Bellasis, too, the petulance of youth had passed: he was discreet, perhaps exemplary. The scandal of his early conduct was unknown to most of the new generation, condoned by the few survivors who had witnessed it.

On the night of November 2nd, 1766, a terrible event revived in the older inhabitants of the College the memory of those evil days. From ten o'clock to midnight a hideous uproar went on in the chamber of Bellasis. Who were his companions none knew. Blasphemous outcries and ribald songs, such as had not been heard for twenty years past, aroused from sleep or study the occupants of the court; but among the voices was not that of Bellasis. At twelve a sudden silence fell upon the cloisters. But the Master lay awake all night, troubled at the relapse of a respected colleague and the horrible example of libertinism set to his pupils.

In the morning all remained quiet about Bellasis' chamber. When his door was opened, soon after daybreak, the early light creeping through the drawn curtains revealed a strange scene. About the table were drawn seven chairs, but some of them had been overthrown, and the furniture was in chaotic disorder, as after some wild orgy. In the chair at the foot of the table sat the lifeless figure of the Secretary, his head bent over his folded arms, as though he would shield his eyes from some horrible sight. Before him on the table lay pen, ink and the red Minute Book. On the last inscribed page, under the date of November 2nd, were written, for the first time since 1742, the autographs of the seven members of the Everlasting Club, but without address. In the same strong hand in which the President's name was written there was appended below the signatures the note, "Mulctatus per Presidentem propter neglectum obsonii, Car. Bellasis."

The Minute Book was secured by the Master of the College, and I believe that he alone was acquainted with the nature of its contents.

The scandal reflected on the college by circumstances revealed in it caused him to keep the knowledge rigidly to himself. But some suspicion of the nature of the occurrences must have percolated to students and servants, for there was a long-abiding belief in the college that, annually on the night of November 2, sounds of unholy revelry were heard to issue from the chamber of Bellasis. I cannot learn that the occupants of the adjoining rooms have ever been disturbed by them. Indeed, it is plain from the minutes that owing to their improvident drafting no provision was made for the perpetuation of the All Souls entertainment after the last Everlasting ceased to be Corporeal. Such superstitious belief must be treated with contemptuous incredulity. But whether for that cause or another the rooms were shut up, and have remained tenantless from that day to this.

The Treasure of John Badcoke

As this narrative of an occurrence in the history of Jesus College may appear to verge on the domain of romance, I think it proper to state by way of preface, that for some of its details I am indebted to documentary evidence which is accessible and veracious. Other portions of the story are supplied from sources the credibility of which my readers will be able to estimate.

On the 8th of November, 1538, the Priory of St. Giles and St. Andrew, Barnwell, was surrendered to King Henry VIII by John Badcoke, the Prior, and the convent of that house. The surrender was sealed with the common seal, subscribed by the Prior and six canons, and acknowledged on the same day in the Chapter House of the Priory, before Thomas Legh, Doctor of Laws[1].

Dr Legh and his fellows, who had been deputed by Cromwell to visit the monasteries, had too frequent occasion to deplore the forwardness of religious households in opposing the King's will in the matter of their dissolution. Among many such reports I need only cite the case of the Prior of Christ Church, Canterbury, mentioned in a letter to Cromwell from one of his agents, Christopher Leyghton[2]. He tells Cromwell that in an inventory exhibited by the Prior to Dr Leyghton, the King's visitor, the Prior had "wilfullye left owte a remembraunce of certayne parcells of silver, gold and stone to the value of thowsandys of poundys"; that it was not to be doubted that he would "eloyne owt of the same howse into the handys of his secret fryndys thowsandes of poundes, which is well knowne he hathe, to hys comfort hereafter"; and that it was common report in the monastery that any monk who should open the matter to the King's advisers "shalbe poysenyde or murtheryde, as he hath murthredde diverse others".

Far different from the truculent attitude of this murderous Prior was the conduct on the like occasion of Prior John Badcoke. Dr Legh reported him to be "honest and conformable". He furnished an exact inventory of the possessions of his house, and quietly retired on the pittance allowed to him by the King. He prevailed upon the other canons to shew the same submission to the royal will, and they peaceably dispersed, some to country incumbencies, others to resume in the Colleges the studies commenced in earlier life.

---

[1] *Cooper, Annals, I., p. 393*
[2] *The Suppression of the Monasteries (Camden Society's Publications), p. 90*

The Treasure of John Badcoke

Oriel Window of Hall & Entrance to 'K' Staircase

John Badcoke settled in Jesus College. The Bursar's Rental of 1538–39 shows that his residence there began in the autumn of the earlier year, immediately after the surrender of the monastery. Divorced from the Priory he was still attached to Barnwell, and took up the duties of Vicar of the small parish church of St. Andrew, which stood close to the Priory gate. So long as Henry VIII lived, and the rites of the old religion were tolerated, he seems to have ministered faithfully to the spiritual needs of his parishioners, unsuspected and unmolested.

More than twelve months elapsed before the demolition of the canons' house was taken in hand, and, for so long, in the empty church the Prior still offered mass on ceremonial days for the repose of the souls of the Peverels and Peches who had built and endowed the house in long bygone days, and were buried beside the High Altar. In the porter's lodge remained the only occupant of the monastery – a former servant of the house, who, from the circumstance that in his secular profession he was a mason, had the name of Adam Waller. Occasional intruders on the solitude of the cloister or the monastic garden sometimes lighted on the ex-Prior pacing the grass-grown walks, as of old, and generally in company with a younger priest.

This companion was named Richard Harrison. He was not one of the dispossessed canons, but came from the Priory of Christ Church, Canterbury, of which mentioned has been made. He was the youngest and latest professed of the monks there, a nephew of the prior, as also of John Badcoke. He had not been present at the time of

Dr Leyghton's visitation, as he happened then to be ejected in his absence he had remained at Barnwell, and there he shared his uncle's parochial duties. He, too, became a resident at Jesus, and he occupied rooms in the College immediately beneath those of Badcoke.

Late in the year 1539 the demolition of Barnwell Priory was begun. Adam Waller was engaged in the work. One incident, which apparently passed almost unnoticed at the time, may be mentioned in connection with this business. The keys of the church were in the keeping of Waller, who had been in the habit of surrendering them to the two ecclesiastics whenever they performed the divine offices there. On the morning when the demolition was to begin, it was found that the stone covering the altar-tomb of Pain Peverel, crusader and founder of the Priory, had been dislodged, and that the earth within it had been recently disturbed. Waller professed to know nothing of the matter.

The account rolls of the College Bursars in the reigns of Henry VIII and Edward VI fortunately tell us exactly the situation of the rooms occupied by Badcoke and Harrison, and as, for the proper understanding of subsequent events, it is necessary that we should realise their condition and relation to the rest of the College, I shall not scruple to be particular. They were on the left-hand side of the staircase now called K, in the eastern range of the College, and at the northern end of what had once been the dormitory of the Nuns of St. Radegund. Badcoke's chamber, which was on the highest floor, was one of the largest in the College, and for that reason the Statutes prescribed that it should be reserved "for more venerable persons resorting to the College"; and Badcoke, being neither a Fellow nor a graduate, was regarded as belonging to this class. Below his chamber was that of Harrison, and on the ground-floor was the 'cool-house', where the College fuel was kept. Between this ground-floor room and L staircase — which did not then exist — there is seen at the present day a rarely opened door. Inside the door a flight of some half-dozen steps descends to a narrow space, which might be deemed a passage, save that it had no outlet at the farther end. On either side it is flanked, to the height of two floors of K staircase, by walls of ancient monastic masonry; the third and highest floor is carried over it. Here, in the times of Henry VIII and the Nunnery days before them, ran or stagnated a Stygian stream, known as "the kytchynge sinke ditch", foul with scum from the College offices. Northward from Badcoke's staircase was "the wood-yard", on the site of the present L staircase. It communicated by a door in its outward, eastern wall with a green close which in the old days had been the Nunnery graveyard. In Badcoke's times it was still uneven with the hillocks which marked the resting-places of nameless, unrecorded Nuns. The old graveyard was intersected by a cart-track leading from Jesus Lane to the wood-yard door. The Bursar's books show that Badcoke controlled the wood-yard and coal-house, perhaps in the capacity of Promus, or Steward.

Now when Badcoke and Harrison came to occupy their chambers on K staircase, Jesus, like other Colleges in those troublous times, had fallen on evil days. Its occupants comprised only the Master, some eight Fellows, a few servants, and about half-a-dozen "disciples".

Nearly half the rooms in College were empty, and the records show that many were tenantless, *propter defectum reparacionis*; that is, because walls, roofs and floors were decayed and ruinous. Badcoke, being a man of means, paid a handsome rent for his chambers, not less than ten shillings by the year, in consideration of which the College put it in tenantable repair; and, as a circumstance which has some significance in relation to this narrative, it is to be noted that the Bursar — the accounts of the year are no longer extant — recorded that in 1539 he paid a sum of three shillings and fourpence "to Adam Waller for layyinge of new brick in ye cupboard of Mr Badcoke's chamber". The cupboard in question was seemingly a small recessed space, still recognisable in a gyp-room belonging to the chambers which were Badcoke's. The rooms on the side of the staircase opposite to those of Badcoke and Harrison were evidently unoccupied; the Bursar took no rent from them. The other inmates of the College dwelt in the cloister court.

In this comparative isolation Badcoke and Harrison lived until the death of Henry VIII in 1546. In course of time Harrison became a Fellow of the College; but Badcoke preferred to retain the exceptional status of its honoured guest. To the Master, Dr Reston, and the Fellows, whose religious sympathies were with the old order of things, their company was inoffensive and even welcome. But trouble came upon the College in 1549, when it was visited by King Edward's Protestant Commissioners. It stands on record, that on May 26th "they commanded six altars to be pulled down in the church", and in a chamber, which may have been Badcoke's, "caused certayn images to be broken". Mr Badcoke "had an excommunicacion sette uppe for him", and was dismissed from the office, whatever it was, that he held in the College. Worse still for his happiness, his companion of many years, Richard Harrison, was "expulsed his felowshippe" on some supposition of trafficking with the court of Rome[1]. He went overseas, as it was understood, to the Catholic University of Louvain in Flanders.

In 1549 Badcoke must have been, as age went in the sixteenth century, an old man. His deprivation of office, the loss of his friend, and the abandonment of long treasured hopes for the restitution of the religious system to which his life had been devoted, plunged him in a settled despondency. The Fellows, who showed for him such sympathy as they dared, understood that between him and Harrison there passed a secret correspondence. But in course of years this source of consolation dried up. Harrison was dead, or he had travelled away from Louvain. With the other members of the College Badcoke wholly parted company, and lived a recluse in his unneighboured room. By the wood-yard gate, of which he still had a key, he could let himself out beyond the College walls, and sometimes by day, oftener after nightfall, he was to be seen wandering beneath his window in the Nuns' graveyard, his old feet, like Friar Laurence's, "stumbling at graves". An occasional visitor, who was known to be his pensioner, was Adam Waller. But, though Waller was still at times employed in the service of the College, his character and condition

---

[1] *Cooper, Annals, II. p. 29*

had deteriorated with years. He was a sturdy beggar, a drunkard, sullen and dangerous in his cups, and Badcoke was heard to hint some terror of his presence. At last the Master learnt from the ex-Prior that he was about to quit the College, and none doubted that he would follow Harrison to Louvain.

Shortly after this became known, Badcoke disappeared from College. He had lived in such seclusion that for a day or two it was not noticed that his door remained closed, and that he had not been seen in his customary walks. When the door was at last forced it was discovered that he had indeed gone, but, strangely, he had left behind the whole of his effects. Adam Waller was the last person who was known to have entered his chamber, and, being questioned, he said that Badcoke had informed him of his intention to depart three days previously, but, for some unexplained reason, had desired him to keep his purpose secret, and had not imparted his destination. Badcoke's life of seclusion, and his known connection with English Catholics beyond sea, gave colour to Waller's story, and, so far as I am aware, no enquiries were made as to the subsequent fate of the ex-Prior. But a strange fact was commented on — that the floor of the so-called cupboard was strewn with bricks, and that in the place from which they had been dislodged was an arched recess of considerable size, which must have been made during Badcoke's tenancy of the room. There was nothing in the recess. Another circumstance there was which called for no notice in the then dilapidated state of half the College rooms. Two boards were loose in the floor of the larger chamber. Thirty feet below the gap which their removal exposed, lay the dark impurities of the "kytchynge sinke ditch".

Adam Waller died a beggar as he had lived.

A century after these occurrences – in the year 1642 – the attention of the College was drawn by a severe visitation of plague to a much-needed sanitary reform. The black ditch which ran under K staircase was "cast", that is, its bed was effectually cleaned out, and its channel was stopped; and so it came about that from that day to this it has presented a clean and dry floor of gravel. Beneath the settled slime of centuries was discovered a complete skeleton. How it came there nobody knew, and nobody enquired. Probably it was guessed to be a relic of some dim and grim monastic mystery.

Now whether Adam Waller knew or suspected the existence of a treasure hidden in the wall-recess of Badcoke's chamber, and murdered the ex-Prior when he was about to remove it to Louvain, I cannot say. One thing is certain – that he did not find the treasure there. When Badcoke disappeared he left his will, with his other belongings, in his chamber. After a decent interval, when it seemed improbable that he would return, probate was obtained by the Master and Fellows, to whom he had bequeathed the chief part of his effects. In 1858 the wills proved in the University court were removed to Peterborough, and there, for aught I know, his will may yet be seen. The property bequeathed consisted principally of books of theology. Among them was Stephanus' Latin Vulgate Bible of 1528 in two volumes folio. This he devised "of my heartie good wylle to my trustie felow and frynde, Richard Harrison, if he shal returne to Cambrege aftyr the tyme of my decesse". Richard Harrison never

The Treasure of John Badcoke

Old Hall, Master's Lodge.

returned to Cambridge, and the Bible, with the other books, found its way to the College Library.

Now there are still in the Library two volumes of this Vulgate Bible. There is nothing in either of them to identify them with the books mentioned in Badcoke's will, for they have lost the fly-leaves which might have revealed the owner's autograph. Here and there in the margins are annotations in a sixteenth-century handwriting; and in the same handwriting on one of the lost leaves was a curious inscription, which suggests that the writer's mind was running on some treasure which was not spiritual. First at the top of the page, in clear and large letters, was copied a passage from Psalm 55: "Cor meum conturbatum est in me: et formido mortis cecidit super me. Et dixi, Quis dabit pennas mihi sicut columbae, et volabo et requiescam." (My heart is disquieted within me: and the fear of death is fallen upon me. And I said, O that I had wings like a dove: for then would I fly away, and be at rest.) Then, in lettering of the same kind, came a portion of Deuteronomy xxviii. 12: "Aperiet dominus thesaurum suum, benedicetque cunctis operibus tuis." (The Lord will disclose his treasure, and will bless all the works of thy hands.) Under this, in smaller letters, were the words, "Vide super hoc Ezechielis cap. xl."

If in the same volume the chapter in question is referred to, a singular fact discloses itself. Certain words in the text are underscored in red pencil, and fingers, inked in the margin, are directed to the lines in which they occur. Taken in their consecutive order these words run: "Ecce murus forinsecus... ad portam quae respiciebat viam orientalem... mensus est a facie portae extrinsecus ad orientem et aquilonem quinque cubitorum... hoc est gazophylacium." This may be taken to mean, "Look at the outside wall... at the gate facing towards the eastern road... he measured from the gate outwards five cubits (7½ feet) towards the north-east... there is the treasure."

The outer wall of the College, the wood-yard gate and the road through the Nuns' cemetery must at once have suggested themselves to Richard Harrison, had he lived to see his friend's bequest, and he must have taken it as an instruction from the testator that a treasure known to both parties was hidden in the spot indicated, close to Badcoke's chamber. And the first text cited must have conveyed to him that his friend, in some deadly terror, had transferred the treasure thither from the place where the two friends had originally laid it. But the message never reached Harrison, and it is quite certain that no treasure has been sought or found in that spot. If the Canterbury or any other treasure was deposited there by Badcoke it rests there still.

To those who are curious to know more of this matter I would say: first, ascertain minutely from Loggan's seventeenth-century plan of the College the position of the wood-yard gate; and, secondly, which indeed should be firstly, make absolutely certain that John Badcoke was not mystifying posterity by an elaborate jest.

The True History of Anthony Ffryar

THE WORLD, IT is said, knows nothing of its greatest men. In our Cambridge microcosm it may be doubted whether we are better informed concerning some of the departed great ones who once walked the confines of our Colleges. Which of us has heard of Anthony Ffryar of Jesus? History is dumb respecting him. Yet but for the unhappy event recorded in this unadorned chronicle his fame might have stood with that of Bacon of Trinity, or Harvey of Caius. *They* lived to be old men: Ffryar died before he was thirty – his work unfinished, his fame unknown even to his contemporaries.

So meagre is the record of his life's work that it is contained in a few bare notices in the college Bursar's Books, in the Grace Books

North West Corner of Cloisters.

which date his matriculation and degrees, and in the entry of his burial on the register of All Saints' Parish. These simple annals I have ventured to supplement with details of a more or less hypothetical character which will serve to show what humanity lost by his early death. Readers will be able to judge for themselves the degree of care which I have taken not to import into the story anything which may savour of the improbable or romantic.

Anthony Ffryar matriculated in the year 1541–2, his age being then probably 15 or 16. He took his B.A. degree in 1545, his M.A. in 1548. He became a Fellow about the end of 1547, and died in the summer of 1551. Such are the documentary facts relating to him. Dr Reston was Master of the College during the whole of his tenure of a Fellowship and died in the same year as Ffryar. The chamber which Ffryar occupied as a Fellow was on the first floor of the staircase at the west end of the Chapel. The staircase has since been absorbed in the Master's Lodge, but the doorway through which it was approached from the cloister may still be seen. At the time when Ffryar lived there the nave of the Chapel was used as a parish church, and his windows overlooked the graveyard then called "Jesus churchyard," which is now a part of the Master's garden.

Ffryar was of course a priest, as were nearly all the Fellows in his day. But I do not gather that he was a theologian, or complied more than formally with the obligation of his orders. He came to Cambridge when the Six Articles and the suppression of the monasteries were of fresh and burning import. He became a Fellow in the harsh Protestant days of Protector Somerset, and in all his time the Master and the Fellows were in scarcely disavowed sympathy with the rites and beliefs of the Old Religion. Yet in the battle of creeds I imagine that he took no part and no interest. I should suppose that he was a somewhat solitary man, an insatiable student of Nature, and that his sympathies with humanity were starved by his absorption in the New Science which dawned on Cambridge at the Reformation.

When I say that he was an alchemist do not suppose that in the middle of the sixteenth century the name of alchemy carried with it any associations with credulity or imposture. It was a real science and a subject of University study then, as its god-children, Physics and Chemistry, are now. If the aims of its professors were transcendental its methods were genuinely based on research. Ffryar was no visionary, but a man of sense, hard and practical. To the study of alchemy he was drawn by no hopes of gain, not even of fame, and still less by any desire to benefit mankind. He was actuated solely by the unquenchable passion for enquiry, a passion sterilizing to all other feeling. To the somnambulisms of the less scientific disciples of his school, such as the philosopher's stone and the elixir of life, he showed himself a chill agnostic. All his thought and energies were concentrated on the discovery of the *magisterium*, the master-cure of all human ailments.

For four years in his laboratory in the cloister he had toiled at this pursuit. More than once, when it had seemed most near, it had eluded his grasp; more than once he had been tempted to abandon it as a mystery insoluble. In the summer of 1551 the discovery waited at his door. He was sure, certain of success, which only experiment could prove. And with the certainty arose a new passion in his heart — to make the name of Ffryar glorious in the healing profession as that of Galen or Hippocrates. In a few days, even within a few hours, the fame of his discovery would go out into all the world.

The summer of 1551 was a sad time in Cambridge. It was marked by a more than usually fatal outbreak of the epidemic called "the sweat," when, as Fuller says, "patients ended or mended in twenty-four hours". It had smouldered some time in the town before it first appeared with sudden and dreadful violence in Jesus College. The first to go was little Gregory Graunge, schoolboy and chorister, who was lodged in the College school in the outer court. He was barely thirteen years old, and known by sight to Anthony Ffryar. He died on July 31, and was buried the same day in Jesus churchyard. The service for his burial was held in the Chapel and at night, as was customary in those days. Funerals in College were no uncommon events in the sixteenth century. But in the death of a poor child, among strangers, there was something to move even the cold heart of Ffryar. And not the pity of it only impressed him. The dim Chapel, the Master and Fellows obscurely ranged in their stalls and shrouded in their hoods, the long-drawn miserable chanting and the childish trebles of the boys who had been Gregory's fellows struck a chill into him which was not to be shaken off.

Three days passed and another chorister died. The College gates were barred and guarded, and, except by a selected messenger, communication with the town was cut off. The precaution was unavailing, and the boys' usher, Mr Stevenson, died on August 5. One of the junior Fellows, sir Stayner – "sir" being the equivalent of B.A. – followed on August 7. The Master, Dr Reston, died the next day. A gaunt, severe man was Dr Reston, whom his Fellows feared. The death of a Master of Arts on August 9 for a time completed the melancholy list.

Before this the frightened Fellows had taken action. The scholars were dismissed to their homes on August 6. Some of the Fellows abandoned the College at the same time. The rest – a terrified conclave – met on August 8 and decreed that the College should be closed until the pestilence should have abated. Until that time it was to be occupied by a certain Robert Laycock, who was a College servant, and his only communication with the outside world was to be through his son, who lived in Jesus Lane. The decree was perhaps the result of the Master's death, for he was not present at the meeting.

Goodman Laycock, as he was commonly called, might have been the sole tenant of the College but for the unalterable decision of Ffryar to remain there. At all hazards his research, now on the eve of realisation, must proceed; without the aid of his laboratory in College it would miserably hang fire. Besides, he had an absolute assurance of his own immunity if the experiment answered his confident expectations, and his fancy was elated with the thought of standing, like another Aaron, between the living and the dead, and staying the pestilence with the potent *magisterium*. Until then he would bar his door even against Laycock, and his supplies of food should be left on his staircase landing. Solitude for him was neither unfamiliar nor terrible.

The True History of Anthony Ffryar

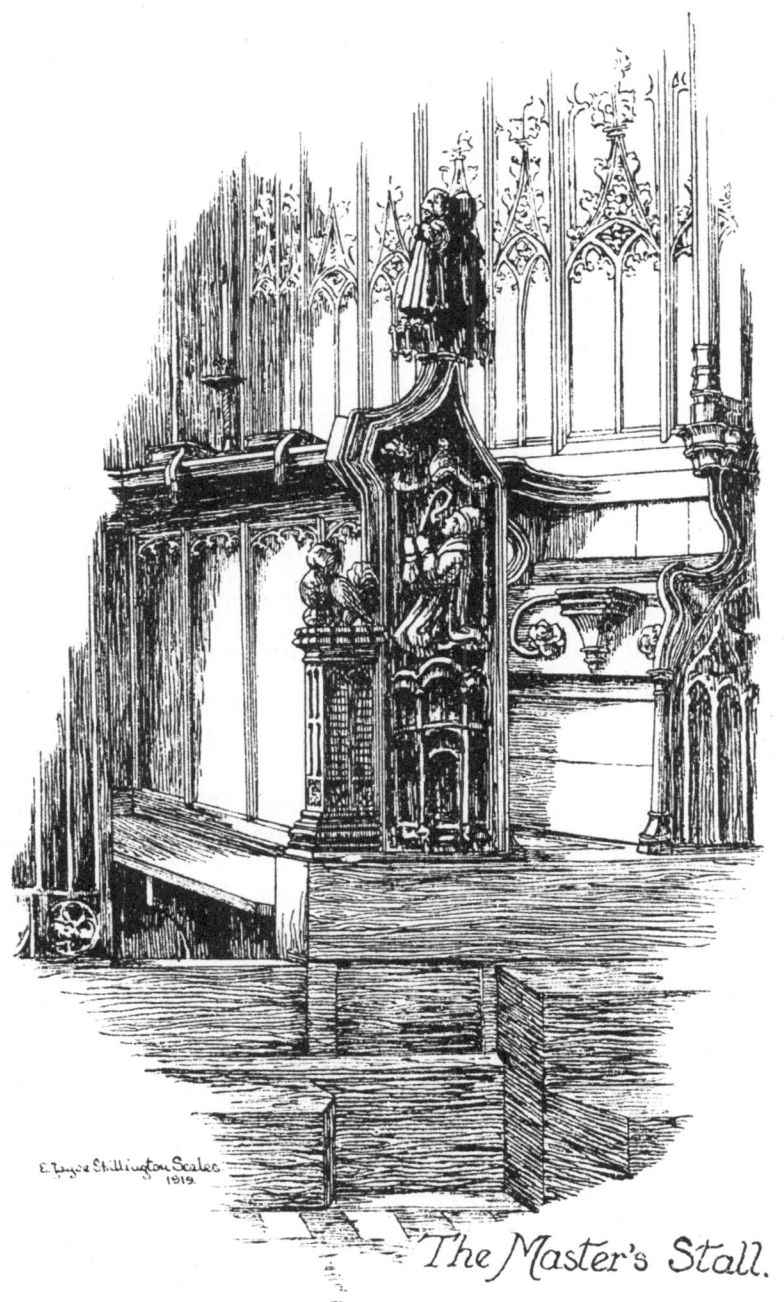

The Master's Stall.

So for three days Ffryar and Laycock inhabited the cloister, solitary and separate. For three days, in the absorption of his research, Ffryar forgot fear, forgot the pestilence-stricken world beyond the gate, almost forgot to consume the daily dole of food laid outside his door. August 12 was the day, so fateful to humanity, when his labours were to be crowned with victory: before midnight the secret of the *magisterium* would be solved.

Evening began to close in before he could begin the experiment which was to be his last. It must of necessity be a labour of some hours, and, before it began, he bethought him that he had not tasted food since early morning. He unbarred his door and looked for the expected portion. It was not there. Vexed at the remissness of Laycock he waited for a while and listened for his approaching footsteps. At last he took courage and descended to the cloister. He called for Laycock, but heard no response. He resolved to go as far as the buttery door and knock. Laycock lived and slept in the Buttery.

At the Buttery door he beat and cried on Laycock; but in answer he heard only the sound of scurrying rats. He went to the window, by the hatch, where he knew that the old man's bed lay, and called to him again. Still there was silence. At last he resolved to force himself through the unglazed window and take what food he could find. In the deep gloom within he stumbled and almost fell over a low object, which he made out to be a truckle-bed. There was light enough from the window to distinguish, stretched upon it, the form of Goodman Laycock, stark and dead.

Sickened and alarmed Ffryar hurried back to his chamber.

More than ever he must hasten the great experiment. When it was ended his danger would be past, and he could go out into the town to call the buryers for the old man. With trembling hands he lit the brazier which he used for his experiments, laid it on his hearth and placed thereon the alembic which was to distil the *magisterium*.

Then he sat down to wait. Gradually the darkness thickened and the sole illuminant of the chamber was the wavering flame of the brazier. He felt feverish and possessed with a nameless uneasiness which, for all his assurance, he was glad to construe as fear: better that than sickness. In the college and the town without was a deathly silence, stirred only by the sweltering of the distilment, and, as the hours struck, by the beating of the Chapel clock, last wound by Laycock. It was as though the dead man spoke. But the repetition of the hours told him that the time of his emancipation was drawing close.

Whether he slept I do not know. He was aroused to vivid consciousness by the clock sounding one. The time when his experiment should have ended was ten, and he started up with a horrible fear that it had been ruined by his neglect. But it was not so. The fire burnt, the liquid simmered quietly, and so far all was well.

Again the College bell boomed a solitary stroke: then a pause and another. He opened, or seemed to open, his door and listened. Again the knell was repeated. His mind went back to the night when he had attended the obsequies of the boy-chorister. This must be a funeral tolling. For whom? He thought with a shudder of the dead man in the Buttery.

He groped his way cautiously down the stairs. It was a still, windless night, and the cloister was dark as death. Arrived at the further side of the court he turned towards the Chapel. Its panes were faintly lighted from within. The door stood open and he entered.

In the place familiar to him at the chancel door one candle flickered on a bracket. Close to it – his face cast in deep shade by the light from behind – stood the ringer, in a gown of black, silent and absorbed in his melancholy task. Fear had almost given way to wonder in the heart of Ffryar, and, as he passed the sombre figure on his way to the chancel door, he looked him resolutely in the face. The ringer was Goodman Laycock.

Ffryar passed into the choir and quietly made his way to his accustomed stall. Four candles burnt in the central walk about a figure laid on the trestles and draped in a pall of black. Two choristers – one on either side – stood by it. In the dimness he could distinguish four figures, erect in the stalls on the other side of the Chapel. Their faces were concealed by their hoods, but in the tall form which occupied the Master's seat it was not difficult to recognise Dr Reston.

The bell ceased and the service began. With some faint wonder Ffryar noted that it was the proscribed Roman Mass for the Dead. The solemn introit was uttered in the tones of Reston, and in the deep responses of the nearest cowled figure he recognised the voice of Stevenson, the usher. None of the mourners seemed to notice Ffryar's presence.

The dreary ceremony drew to a close. The four occupants of the stalls descended and gathered round the palled figure in the aisle.

With a mechanical impulse, devoid of fear or curiosity, and with a half-prescience of what he should see, Anthony Ffryar drew near and uncovered the dead man's face. He saw — himself.

At the same moment the last wailing notes of the office for the dead broke from the band of mourners, and, one by one, the choristers extinguished the four tapers.

"Requiem aeternam dona ei, Domine," chanted the hooded four: and one candle went out.

"Et lux perpetua luceat ei," was the shrill response of the two choristers: and a second was extinguished.

"Cum sanctis tuis in aeternum," answered the four: and one taper only remained.

The Master threw back his hood, and turned his dreadful eyes straight upon the living Anthony Ffryar: he threw his hand across the bier and held him tight. "Cras tu eris mecum[1]," he muttered, as if in antiphonal reply to the dirge-chanters.

With a hiss and a sputter the last candle expired.

The hiss and the sputter and a sudden sense of gloom recalled Ffryar to the waking world. Alas for labouring science, alas for the fame of Ffryar, alas for humanity, dying and doomed to die! The vessel containing the wonderful brew which should have redeemed the world had fallen over and dislodged its contents on the fire below.

---

[1] Samuel xxvii. 19

An accident reparable, surely, within a few hours; but not by Anthony Ffryar. How the night passed with him no mortal can tell. All that is known further of him is written in the register of All Saints' Parish. If you can discover the ancient volume containing the records of the year 1551 — and I am not positive that it now exists — you will find it written:

>Die Augusti xiii
>>Buryalls in Jhesus churchyarde
>>>Goodman Laycock — Of ye sicknesse
>>>Anthony Ffryar — Of ye sicknesse

Whether he really died of "the sweat" I cannot say. But that the living man was sung to his grave by the dead, who were his sole companions in Jesus College, on the night of August 12, 1551, is as certain and indisputable as any other of the facts which are here set forth in the history of Anthony Ffryar.

The Necromancer

HIS IS A story of Jesus College, and it relates to the year 1643. In that year Cambridge town was garrisoned for the Parliament by Colonel Cromwell and the troops of the Eastern Counties' Association. Soldiers were billeted in all the colleges, and contemporary records testify to their violent behaviour and the damage which they committed in the chambers which they occupied. In the previous year the Master of Jesus College, Doctor Sterne, was arrested by Cromwell when he was leaving the chapel, conveyed to London, and there imprisoned in the Tower. Before the summer of 1643 fourteen of the sixteen Fellows were expelled, and during the whole of that year there were, besides the soldiers, only some ten or

twelve occupants of the college. The names of the two Fellows who were not ejected were John Boyleston and Thomas Allen.

With Mr Boyleston this history is only concerned for the part which he took on the occasion of the visit to the college of the notorious fanatic, William Dowsing. Dowsing came to Cambridge in December 1642, armed with powers to put in execution the ordinance of Parliament for the reformation of churches and chapels. Among the devastations committed by this ignorant clown, and faithfully recorded by him in his diary, it stands on record that on December 28, in the presence and perhaps with the approval of John Boyleston, he "digg'd up the steps (*i.e.* of the altar) and brake down Superstitions and Angels, 120 at the least." Dowsing's account of his proceedings is supplemented by the Latin History of the college, written in the reign of Charles II by one of the Fellows, a certain Doctor John Sherman. Sherman records, but Dowsing does not, that there was a second witness of the desecration – Thomas Allen. Of the two he somewhat enigmatically remarks: "The one (*i.e.* Boyleston) stood behind a curtain to witness the evil work: the other, afflicted to behold the exequies of his Alma Mater, made his life a filial offering at her grave, and, to escape the hands of wicked rebels, laid violent hands on himself."

That Thomas Allen committed suicide seems a fairly certain fact: and that remorse for the part which he had unwillingly taken in the sacrilege of December 28 prompted his act we may accept on the testimony of Sherman. But there is something more to tell which Sherman either did not know or did not think fit to record.

His book deals only with the college and its society. He had no occasion to remember Adoniram Byfield.

Byfield was a chaplain attached to the Parliamentary forces in Cambridge, and quarters were assigned to him in Jesus College, in the first floor room above the gate of entrance. Below his chamber was the Porter's lodge, which at that time served as the armoury of the troopers who occupied the college. Above it, on the highest floor of the gate-tower "kept" Thomas Allen. These were the only rooms on the staircase. At the beginning of the Long Vacation of 1643 Allen was the only member of the college who continued to reside.

Some light is thrown on the character of Byfield and his connection with this story by a pudgy volume of old sermons of the Commonwealth period which is contained in the library of the college. Among the sermons which are bound up in it is one which bears the date 1643 and is designated on the title page:

> A FAITHFUL ADMONICION of the Baalite sin of *Enchanters & Stargazers*, preacht to the Colonel Cromwell's Souldiers in Saint Pulcher's (*i.e.* Saint Sepulchre's) church, in Cambridge, by the fruitfull Minister, *Adoniram Byfield*, late departed unto God, in the yeare 1643, touching that of *Acts* the seventh, verse 43, *Ye took up the Tabernacle of Moloch, the Star of your god Remphan, figures which ye made to worship them; & I will carrie you away beyond Babylon.*

Tedious Brief Tales of Granta & Gramarye

Main Gateway
& Porter's Lodge

The discourse, in its title as in its contents, reveals its author as one of the fanatics who wrought on the ignorance and prejudice against "carnal" learning which actuated the Cromwellian soldiers in their brutal usage of the University "scholars" in 1643. All Byfield's learning was contained in one book — *the* Book. For him the revelation which gave it sufficed for its interpretation. What needed Greek to the man who spoke mysteries in unknown tongues, or the light of comment to him who was carried in the spirit into the radiance of the third heaven?

Now Allen, too, was an enthusiast, lost in mystic speculation. His speculation was in the then novel science of mathematics and astronomy. Even to minds not darkened by the religious mania that possessed Byfield, that science was clouded with suspicion in the middle of the seventeenth century. Anglican, Puritan, and Catholic were agreed in regarding its great exponent, Descartes, as an atheist. Mathematicians were looked upon as necromancers, and Thomas Hobbes says that in his days at Oxford the study was considered to be "smutched with the black art," and fathers, from an apprehension of its malign influence, refrained from sending their sons to that University. How deep the prejudice had sunk into the soul of Adoniram as his sermon shows. The occasion which suggested it was this. A pious cornet, leaving a prayer-meeting at night, fell down one of the steep, unlighted staircases of the college and broke his neck. Two or three of the troopers were taken with a dangerous attack of dysentery. There was talk of these misadventures among the soldiers, who somehow connected them with Allen and his studies.

The floating gossip gathered into a settled conviction in the mind of Adoniram.

For Allen was a mysterious person. Whether it was because he was engrossed in his studies, or that he shrank from exposing himself to the insults of the soldiers, he seldom showed himself outside his chamber. Perhaps he was tied to it by the melancholy to which Sherman ascribed his violent end. In his three months' sojourn on Allen's staircase Byfield had not seen him a dozen times, and the mystery of his closed door awakened the most fantastic speculations in the chaplain's mind. For hours together, in the room above, he could hear the mumbled tones of Allen's voice, rising and falling in ceaseless flow. No answer came, and no word that the listener could catch conveyed to his mind any intelligible sense. Once the voice was raised in a high key and Byfield distinctly heard the ominous ejaculation, "Avaunt Sathanas, avaunt!" Once through his partly open door he had caught sight of him standing before a board chalked with figures and symbols which the imagination of Byfield interpreted as magical. At night, from the court below, he would watch the astrologer's lighted window, and when Allen turned his perspective glass upon the stars the conviction became rooted in his watcher's mind that he was living in perilous neighbourhood to one of the peeping and muttering wizards of whom the Holy Book spoke.

An unusual occurrence strengthened the suspicions of Byfield. One night he heard Allen creep softly down the staircase past his room; and, opening the door, he saw him disappear round the staircase foot, candle in hand. Silently, in the dark, Byfield followed him and saw him pass into the Porter's lodge. The soldiers were in bed and the armoury was unguarded. Through the lighted pane he saw Allen take down a horse-pistol from a rack on the wall. He examined it closely, tried the lock, poised it as if to take aim, then replaced it and, leaving the lodge, disappeared up the staircase with his candle. A world of suspicions rushed on Byfield's mind, and they were not allayed when the soldiers reported in the morning that the pistols were intact. But one of the sick soldiers died that week.

Brooding on this incident Adoniram became more than ever convinced of the Satanic purposes and powers of his neighbour, and his suspicions were confirmed by another mysterious circumstance. As the weeks passed he became aware that at a late hour of night Allen's door was quietly opened. There followed a patter of scampering feet down the staircase, succeeded by silence. In an hour or two the sound came back. The patter went up the stairs to Allen's chamber, and then the door was closed. To lie awake waiting for this ghostly sound became a horror to Byfield's diseased imagination. In his bed he prayed and sang psalms to be relieved of it. Then he abandoned thoughts of sleep and would sit up waiting if he might surprise and detect this walking terror of the night. At first in the darkness of the stairs it eluded him. One night, light

On 'O' Staircase

in hand, he managed to get a glimpse of it as it disappeared at the foot of the stairs. It was shaped like a large black cat.

Far from allaying his terrors, the discovery awakened new questionings in the heart of Byfield. Quietly he made his way up to Allen's door. It stood open and a candle burnt within. From where he stood he could see each corner of the room. There was the board scribbled with hieroglyphs: there were the magical books open on the table: there were the necromancer's instruments of unknown purpose. But there was no live thing in the room, and no sound save the rustling of papers disturbed by the night air from the open window.

A horrible certitude seized on the chaplain's mind. This Thing that he had caught sight of was no cat. It was the Evil One himself, or it was the wizard translated into animal shape. On what foul errand was he bent? Who was to be his new victim? With a flash there came upon his mind the story how Phinehas had executed judgement on the men that were joined to Baal-peor, and had stayed the plague from the congregation of Israel. He would be the minister of the Lord's vengeance on the wicked one, and it should be counted unto him for righteousness unto all generations for evermore.

He went down to the armoury in the Porter's lodge. Six pistols, he knew, were in the rack on the wall. Strange that to-night there were only five – a fresh proof of the justice of his fears. One of the five he selected, primed, loaded and cocked in readiness for the wizard's return. He took his stand in the shadow of the wall, at the entrance of the staircase. That his aim might be surer he left his candle burning at the stair-foot.

In solemn stillness the minutes drew themselves out into hours while Adoniram waited and prayed to himself. Then in the poring darkness he became sensible of a moving presence, noiseless and unseen. For a moment it appeared in the light of the candle, not two paces distant. It was the returning cat. A triumphant exclamation sprang to Byfield's lips, "God shall shoot at them, suddenly shall they be wounded" – and he fired.

With the report of the pistol there rang through the court a dismal outcry, not human nor animal, but resembling, as it seemed to the excited imagination of the chaplain, that of a lost soul in torment. With a scurry the creature disappeared in the darkness of the court, and Byfield did not pursue it. The deed was done – that he felt sure of – and as he replaced the pistol in the rack a gush of religious exaltation filled his heart. That night there was no return of the pattering steps outside his door, and he slept well.

Next day the body of Thomas Allen was discovered in the grove which girds the college – his breast pierced by a bullet. It was surmised that he had dragged himself thither from the court. There were tracks of blood from the staircase foot, where it was conjectured that he had shot himself, and a pistol was missing from the armoury. Some of the inmates of the court had been aroused by the discharge of the weapon. The general conclusion was that recorded by Sherman – that the fatal act was prompted by brooding melancholy.

Of his part in the night's transactions Byfield said nothing. The grim intelligence, succeeding the religious excitation of the night, brought to him questioning, dread, horror. Whatever others might surmise, he was fatally convinced that it was by his hand that Allen had died. Pity for the dead man had no place in the dark cabin of his soul. But how was it with himself? How should his action be weighed before the awful Throne? His lurid thought pictured the Great Judgement as already begun, the Book opened, the Accuser of the Brethren standing to resist him, and the dreadful sentence of Cain pronounced upon him, "Now art thou cursed from the earth."

In the evening he heard them bring the dead man to the chamber above his own. They laid him on his bed, and, closing the door, left him and descended the stairs. The sound of their footsteps died away and left a dreadful silence. As the darkness grew the horror of the stillness became insupportable. How he yearned that he might hear again the familiar muffled voice in the room above! And in an excess of fervour he prayed aloud that the terrible present might pass from him, that the hours might go back, as on the dial of Ahaz, and all might be as yesterday.

Suddenly, as the prayer died on his lips, the silence was broken. He could not be mistaken. Very quietly he heard Allen's door open, and the old, pattering steps crept softly down the stairs. They passed his door. They were gone before he could rise from his knees to open it. A momentary flash lighted the gloom in Byfield's soul. What if his prayer was heard, if Allen was not dead, if the events of the past twenty-four hours were only a dream and a delusion of the

Wicked One? Then the horror returned intensified. Allen was assuredly dead. This creeping Thing — what might it be?

For an hour in his room Byfield sat in agonised dread. Most, the thought of the open door possessed him like a nightmare. Somehow it must be closed before the foul Thing returned. Somehow the mangled shape within must be barred up from the wicked powers that might possess it. The fancy gripped and stuck to his delirious mind. It was horrible, but it must be done. In a cold terror he opened his door and looked out.

A flickering light played on the landing above. Byfield hesitated. But the thought that the cat might return at any moment gave him a desperate courage. He mounted the stairs to Allen's door. Precisely as yesternight it stood wide open. Inside the room the books, the instruments, the magical figures were unchanged, and a candle, exposed to the night wind from the casement, threw wavering shadows on the walls and floor. At a glance he saw it all, and he saw the bed where, a few hours ago, the poor remains of Allen had been laid. The coverlet lay smooth upon it. The dead necromancer was not there.

Then as he stood, footbound at the door, a wandering breath from the window caught the taper, and with a gasp the flame went out. In the black silence he became conscious of a moving sound. Nearer, up the stairs they drew — the soft creeping steps — and in panic he shrank backwards into Allen's room before their advance.

Already they were on the last flight of the stairs; and then in the doorway the darkness parted and Byfield saw. In a ring of pallid light that seemed to emanate from its body he beheld the cat — horrible, gory, its foreparts hanging in ragged collops from its neck. Slowly it crept into the room, and its eyes, smoking with dull malevolence, were fastened on Byfield. Further he backed into the room, to the corner where the bed was laid. The creature followed. It crouched to spring upon him. He dropped in a sitting posture on the bed and as he saw it launch itself upon him, he closed his eyes and found speech in a gush of prayer, "O my God, make haste for my help." In an agony he collapsed upon the couch and clutched its covering with both hands. Beneath it he gripped the stiffened limbs of the dead necromancer, and, when he opened his eyes, the darkness had returned and the spectral cat was gone.

Brother John's Bequest

N A CERTAIN morning in the summer of the year 1510 John Ecclestone, Doctor in Divinity and Master of Jesus College in Cambridge, stood at the door of his lodge looking onto the cloister court. There was a faint odour of extinguished candles in the air, and a bell automatically clanked in unison with its bearer's step. It was carried by a young acolyte, who lagged in the rear of a small band of white-robed figures who were just disappearing from sight at the corner of the passage leading to the entrance court. They were the five Fellows of the newly-constituted College.

As they disappeared, the Master, with much deliberation, spat into the cloister walk.

To spit behind a man's back might be accounted a mark of disgust, contempt, malice – at least of disapproval. Such were not the feelings of Dr Ecclestone.

It is a fact known all over the world, Christian and heathen, that visitants from the unseen realm cannot endure to be spat at. The Master's action was prophylactic. For supernatural visitings of the transitory, curable kind the rites of the Church are, no doubt, efficacious. In inveterate cases it is well to leave no remedy untried.

With bell, book and candle the Master and Fellows had just completed a lustration of the lodge. The bell had clanked in the Founder's Chamber and in the Master's oratory. The Master's bedchamber had been well soused with holy water. The candle had explored dark places in cupboards and under the stairs. If It was there before it was almost inconceivable that It remained there now. But one cannot be too careful.

Two days previously a funeral had taken place in the College. It was a shabby affair. The deceased, John Baldwin, late a brother of the dissolved Hospital of Saint John, was put away in an obscure part of the College churchyard – now the Master's garden – behind some elder bushes which grew in the corner bounded by the street and the "chimney." The mourners were the grave-digger, the sexton and the parson of All Saints' Church. Though brother John had died in a college chamber the society of Jesus marked its reprobation of his manner of living by absenting themselves from his obsequies.

Brother John had been a disappointment: uncharitable persons might say he was a fraud. He had got into the College by false pretences.

In life he had disgraced it by his excesses, and, when he was dead, he had perpetrated a mean practical joke on the society. It is not well for a man in religious orders to joke when he is dead.

How did it come that brother John Baldwin, late Granger of the Augustinian Hospital of Saint John, died in Jesus College?

The hospital of Saint John was dissolved in the year 1510, to make room for the new college designed by the Lady Margaret. Bishops of Ely for three centuries and more had been its patrons and visitors, and dissolute James Stanley, bishop in 1510, fought stoutly for its maintenance. But circumstances were too strong for the bishop. The ancient Hospital was hopelessly bankrupt. The buildings were ruinous: there was not a doit in the treasury chest: the household goods were pawned to creditors in the town. The Master, William Tomlyn, had disappeared, none knew whither, and only two brethren were left in the place. One of them was John Baldwin: the other was the Infirmarer, a certain Bartholemew Aspelon.

On the eve of the dissolution, bishop Stanley wrote a letter to the Master and Fellows of the other Cambridge society of which he was visitor, namely, Jesus College. He commended to their charitable care brother John Baldwin, an aged man of godly conversation who was disposed to bestow his worldly goods for the comfort and sustenance of the Master and Fellows in consideration of their maintenance of him in College during the remaining years of his earthly pilgrimage. It was a not uncommon practice in those days for monasteries and colleges to accept as inmates persons, clerical or lay, who wished to withdraw from the world and were willing, either during life or by testamentary arrangements, to guarantee their hosts against pecuniary loss.

Report said that, though the Hospital was penniless, brother John in his private circumstances was well-to-do and even affluent. It did not befit the Master and Fellows to enquire how he had come by his wealth. They were wretchedly poor, and the bishop's certificate of character was all that could be desired. They thanked the bishop for his prudent care for their interests and covenanted to give the religious man a domicile in the College with allowance for victuals, barber, laundress, wine, wax and all other things necessary for celebrating Divine service, as to any Fellow of the College. Brother John promptly transferred himself to his new quarters, which were in a room called "the loft," on the top floor above the Founder's Chamber in the Master's lodge.

The Master and Fellows were disappointed in brother John's luggage. It consisted simply of two brass-bound boxes, heavy but unquestionably small, even for a man of religion. An encouraging feature about them was that they bore the monogram of Saint John's Hospital. Brother John and his former co-mate of the Hospital, Bartholemew Aspelon, constantly affirmed that the missing Master, William Tomlyn, had decamped with the contents of the Hospital treasury. But the society of Jesus hoped that they were not telling the truth. Brother John kept the two boxes under his bed. They were always carefully locked, but brother John threw out vague hints that their contents were destined for a princely benefaction to his hospitable entertainers.

In other respects brother John's equipment was not such as would betoken a man of wealth. Rather it savoured of monastical austerity. His only suit of clothing was ancient, and even greasy. It was never changed, night or day. Brother John was apparently under a religious obligation to abstain from washing.

As a man of godly conversation brother John was unfortunate in his personal appearance. It was presumably a stroke of paralysis which had drawn up one side of his face and correspondingly depressed the other. His mouth was a diagonal compromise with the rest of his features. One eye was closed, and the other was bleared and watery. His nose was red, but the rest of his face was of a parchment colour.

Brother John was an elderly person, and continued ill health unfortunately confined him to his chamber, above the Master's. He expressed a deep regret that he could not share the society of the Fellows in the Hall at their meals of oatmeal porridge, salt fish, and thin ale. His distressing ailments necessitated a sustaining diet of capons and oysters, supplied to him in his chamber by the College. He was equally debarred from attending services in the Chapel, but the wine with which the society had covenanted to supply him was punctually consumed at the private offices which he performed in his chamber. A suitable pecuniary compensation was made to him on the ground that his domestic arrangements rendered the services of the College laundress unnecessary.

Bartholemew Aspelon, who lodged in an alehouse in the town, was the constant and affectionate attendant at brother John's sick bed:

for, indeed, he seldom got out of it. From a neighbouring tavern he brought to him abundant supplies of the ypocras and malmsey wine which were requisite for the maintenance of the invalid's failing strength. Brother Bartholemew was an individual of a merry countenance and gifted with cheerful song. In the sick room the Fellows would often hear him trolling a drinking catch, to which the invalid joined a quavering note. So constant and familiar was the lay that John Bale, one of the Fellows, remembered it thirty years afterwards, and put it in the mouth of a roistering monk whom he introduced as one of the characters in his play, *King Johan*. The words ran thus:

> Wassayle, wassayle, out of the mylke payle,
> Wassayle, wassayle, as whyte as my nayle,
> Wassayle, wassayle, in snow, frost and hayle,
> Wassayle, wassayle, with partriche and rayle,
> Wassayle, wassayle, that much doth avayle,
> Wassayle, wassayle, that never wyll fayle.

The invasion of the college silences by this unusual concert was marked by the Fellows with growing disapproval: and they were not comforted when they discovered that the new robe which they had contracted to supply to their guest had been pledged to the host of the Sarazin's Head in part payment of an account rendered. But they possessed their souls in patience as they noted that the health of their venerable guest was declining with obvious rapidity. With some insistence they pointed out to the Master the desirability of having

Fireplace in Master's Lodge.

a prompt and clear understanding about brother John's testamentary dispositions. Dr Eccleston was entirely of the Fellows' mind in the matter.

One evening in June, some three months after brother John had begun his residence in the College, it seemed to Dr Eccleston that the time had come to sound him about his intentions. The patient was very low, and brother Bartholomew was much depressed.

With inkhorn and pen the Master went upstairs to the sick man's chamber. Nuncupatory wills were in those days accepted as legal obligations, and the Master was minded that he would not leave brother John until he had obtained, from his dictation, a statement of his intentions as to the disposal of his goods.

Obviously brother John's mind was wandering when the Master entered the room, for he greeted his arrival with a snatch of the old scurvy tune,

> Wassayle, wassayle, that never wyll fayle,

and feebly added "Art there, bully Bartholomew? Bear me thy hand to the bottle, for I am dry."

"Brother John, brother John," said the Master, "bestir thee, and think of thy state. It is time for thee to consider of thy world's gear and how thou wilt bestow it according to thy promise to our poor company, for their tendance of thee." Brother John raised himself in his bed and opened his serviceable eye. Something like a grin puckered up his sloping mouth. "Art thou of that counsel, goodman

Doctor?" said he: "then have with thee. I were a knave if I did not thank you for your kindness, and, trust me, ye shall not be the losers for your pains. Take quill and write. I will dictate my will in two fillings of thy pen. Write:" and the Master wrote.

"To the Master and Fellows of Jesus College I give and bequeath that chest that lieth beneath my bed and is marked with a great letter A, and all that is in it. To brother Bartholomew Aspelon, late of the Hospital of Saint John, in like manner I bequeath that other chest that is marked B."

"Is that all?" asked the Master. "Gogswouns, it is all I have," said brother John. "Yet stay, good Master. Nothing for nothing is a safe text. Thou shalt write it as a condition, on pain of forfeiting my bequest, that ye shall bury me in the aisle of your church, immediately before the High Altar: that ye shall keep my obit, or anniversary, with *placebo* and *dirige* and mass of requiem; and that once each week a Fellow that is a priest shall pray and sing for the soul of John Baldwin, the benefactor of the College. Is it rehearsed, master doctor?" "It is written," said the Master. "*Ite, missa est*," said the invalid, "and fetch me a stoup of small ale, good Master."

A few days later John Baldwin made his unimproving, un-regretted end. Brother Bartholomew carried off his portion of the legacy. The other chest was deposited on the table in the Founder's Chamber and opened by the Master before the assembled Fellows.

It contained half a dozen bricks, a fair quantity of straw and shavings, and nothing else — nothing except a small scrap of torn and dirty paper at the bottom of the box. With one voice the Master and

Fellows decreed that their unworthy guest should be buried in the least respectable portion of the churchyard. Which thing was done, as I have already mentioned.

Of course the dirty paper under the straw was scrutinized by the Master and Fellows. But it was of no importance. It looked like a deed or a will, in which the deceased, in return for nursing in sickness, proposed to give some unspecified property to his disreputable friend, Aspelon, and apparently stipulated that he should be buried in the choir of the Hospital chapel. But it was not witnessed: it had obviously been torn up, and all that was left of it was the part on the scribe's right hand. It ran thus:

> ego Johnannes Baldewyn nuper frat
> rigiam do lego et confirmo domino
> u pro mea in egritudine relevaci
> domino Bartolomeo Aspelon confrat
> ne quod habeat uter prior invener
> am in tumulo sepultus subter quen
> parte chori in sacello Hospitalis
> theshede

The last word, if rightly read, was unintelligible.

But the College had by no means done with brother John. On the evening after his burial, as the Master and Fellows were leaving the Chapel, their steps were suddenly arrested as they heard the familiar Wassail stave raised in a thin and tuneless voice. It came from the open window of the deceased brother, and unquestionably the voice was not Aspelon's. In consternation they listened till it died ineffectually away in an attempted chorus strain.

After brief deliberation they resolved to visit the "loft" in a body – Master, Fellows, "disciples" and servants – and see what this thing might mean. They found the place as blank and silent as it remained when the deceased had been taken out to his burial. But before they reached the stair-foot in their descent the thin piping strain fell on their ears again, and this time none were bold enough to go back. After that, at all times of the night and day, the interminable ditty was fitfully renewed, and panic held the College. At night the "disciples" huddled in one room, and the Fellows lay two in a bed.

Unfortunately for Dr Eccleston, he was condemned to the solitude of the lodge, deserted even by his *famulus*, the sizar who attended him. He sat up all night and studied works of divinity, in the hope that theology, if it did not put the songster to rout, would at least distract his own thoughts from the devilish roundelay in the garret above his head. On the second night he began to congratulate himself on the success of his experiment, for the singer relapsed into silence. In his exhaustion he might even have slept, but that the door of his study had a gusty habit of flying open unexpectedly and closing with a bang. He had actually begun to drowse over his folio when a sharp pressure on his right shoulder aroused him. Hastily turning his head he saw the papery countenance of the dead brother gazing on him with all the affection that one eye could testify, the chin planted in the Master's shoulder, and the mouth slewed into a simulation of innocent mirth. Dr Eccleston read no more divinity that night.

Early next morning a College meeting was summoned by the Master. It was resolved by the unanimous voice of the society that brother John's remains should be exhumed and re-interred in the middle of the chancel aisle, in accordance with the stipulation of the deceased: and there was no delay in carrying the resolution into effect. The Master also insisted that the whole society should help in the purgation of his lodge and the loft above it, in accordance with the ritual of the Church in that case applying: and this too was incontinently done, as I have already described. The consideration of the performance of the rest of the contract entered into by the Master with the late brother was deferred until it should be ascertained how far the deceased was satisfied with the measures already adopted.

Whether John Baldwin acquiesced in this somewhat lame execution of his wishes, or whether his perturbed spirit was laid to rest by the rites of exorcism it is impossible to say. It is quite certain that he troubled the College no more.

But in the afternoon following his re-interment an incident happened which possibly had some connection with the placation of his shade. Bartholomew Aspelon had not attended brother John's funeral in the churchyard. In truth, he was filled with a moral resentment at his late friend's lack of feeling and good taste which was only equalled by that of the society of Jesus: and the motive was the same. On opening the treasure chest bequeathed to him he had found it filled with bricks and straw, just like the other. If the Fellows were indignant Bartholomew was more so: for, from private sources of information which he possessed as a member of the dissolved Hospital, he was assured that brother John had prospered in its service to the extent of £200, at the least, and he was profoundly convinced that the whole sum had gone into the treasury of Jesus College. Under the straw he had found a morsel of paper, which was, indeed, too fragmentary to give any connected clue to its drift, but which, nevertheless, rather plainly indicated on the part of the deceased an intention of bequeathing to the college a certain treasure, the whereabouts of which, owing to the imperfection of the document, were not stated. He was confirmed in his interpretation of the manuscript by the honourable interment given to brother John's remains in the Chapel.

Filled with resentment at the ingratitude of the patient whom he had so tenderly nursed and at the duplicity of the "dons" who had robbed him of the reward of his devoted service, Bartholomew sought the Master's lodge. He used no language of studied courtesy in representing to Dr Eccleston the nature of his grievance: and the Master, whose temper was severely tried by want of sleep and the disagreeable nature of the interment ceremony in which he had just unwillingly participated, replied with equal vehemence.

"Ye are robbers all," cried Bartholomew: "you cheated him in his weakness into signing away from the friend who smoothed his pillow in his dying hours."

"Thou naughty knave," retorted the Master, "talk not to me of bricks and straw. It was gold that was contained in thy box, and the devil knows by what scurvy arts thou didst cozen us of our promised reward. His own paper convicts thee of the fraudulent attempt to get him to will his goods to thee. See what he left in the bottom of our box." And the Master threw the scrap above-transcribed upon the table. "Take it and never let me see thy rogue's face again."

Brother Bartholomew leaped in his skin as he grabbed the document. He made no ceremony of leave-taking, but bolted down the stairs. When he got into the cloister outside he took from his pouch a dingy scrap of paper, which was the fellow of that which the Master had thrown to him. What he read on it was this:

> Sciant omnes presentes et futuri quod
> er Hospitalis Divi Johannis apud Canteb
> doctori Ecclyston et sociis Collegii Jes
> one equaliter inter se dividendum aut
> ri meo in antedicto Hospitali ea racio
> it totum thesaurum meum ita ut extat cl
> dam lapidem iacentem in septentrionali
> eiusdem cuius istud signum extat a dea

Then brother Bartholomew put the two pieces together, and it was thus that he translated the continuous lines:

Know all men present and to come that | I, John
    Baldwin, late a broth
er of the Hospital of Saint John at Camb | ridge,
    give, grant and bequeath to master
doctor Eccleston and the fellows of the College of
    Jes | u for my relief during sick
ness, equally to be divided among them, or | to
    master Bartholomew Aspelon, a brother
of mine in the aforesaid Hospital, provid | ed that
    he shall have it who is first fin
der, all my treasure as it now lies pri | vily buried in
    a tomb under a cert
ain stone lying on the northern | side of the choir
    in the chapel of the Hospital
aforesaid, of which this is the sign, a dea | th's
    head.

Of what further pertains to brother John Baldwin and his bequest I have no more to say than that his name is not included in the Form for the Commemoration of Benefactors of Jesus College. Also that for twenty years after the events here recorded a cheerful individual, in a lay habit, might be seen, seated of custom on the ale-bench at the Sarazin's Head. He drank of the best, paid in cash and never lacked for money. He could tell a good tale and he sang a good song. His Wassail song was always in request at the Sarazin's Head.

The Burden of Dead Books

Y ITS AIR of reverend quiet, its redolence of dusty death, in the marshalled lines of its sleeping occupants, and in the labels that briefly name the dead author and his work, an ancient repository of books, such as a college library, suggests the, perhaps, hackneyed similitude of a great cemetery. Here and there, among the vast majority of the undistinguished dead, we detect names that are still familiar. Here and there are the monuments of men who have at least been the ancestors of a surviving family of scholars and scientists. Some names will awake memories, not for the individual achievement of their bearers, but for the cause in which they worked. Royalist and Republican, Anglican, Romanist and Puritan here have laid down the

arms which they bore against each other, and together sleep the sleep from which there is no rising. Though the issues for which these men fought are dead things now, their spirit is with us and their works follow them. But with the majority it is not so. Outnumbering all others are the hand-labourers of whose names the catalogue has no record. Their daywork, paid or unpaid, was commanded by more ambitious masters, who absorbed whatever temporary measure of credit attended the collaboration. Over the ashes of these unnamed toilers we waste no regrets: they sleep well. It is the fallen ambitions, the wasted energies, the mistaken aims of the master-craftsmen in letters that are food for ironical contemplation.

I do not know that in such a cemetery of small and great, the servant and his master, a more dismal corner exists than that which is reserved for the stillborn. They are a great host, and they are mostly of the family of Theology. Of one such product of fruitless travail I have to speak. It has rested undisturbed in the library of Jesus College for over 300 years, and in all that time, perhaps, no human being, except the official who transcribed its title in the catalogue, has ever had occasion to recall its existence. Its author was one Matthew Makepeace, S.T.P., a Fellow of the College in the last quarter of the sixteenth century. Its elaborate title is: "Speculum Archimagiae, sive Straguli Babyloniaci Direptio, necnon Offuciarum et Praestigiarum Romano-papisticarum Apocalypsis liberrima", from which I conclude that the Pope received some hard knocks in it, and that the Babylonian lady of the Book of Revelation was left in pitiful disarray by the learned doctor's assault. The title-page informs us that

The Burden of Dead Books

A Corner of the Library.

the book was printed at London by Melchisedeck Bradwell, for John Bill, in the year of 1604: furthermore, that it had been "perused and approved by publike authoritie". That it was ever perused I do not believe. Only in the most cursory way have I perused it myself, and I do not think that any other man has done as much. To our patient ancestors a book was a book, let it be ever so dull. They glossed it, annotated it, added their approving or inimical comments. But nobody has been at the pains to add his marginal notes to the text of Matthew Makepeace. Its cover is unworn, its pages as clean as on the day when it first saw light. This only: on a loose scrap of paper, contained between its pages, I have discovered a name written in Greek characters and a short Greek quotation.

Let me get done with this dull book as fast as I can. It is, of course, written in Latin, and its style does not suggest that the author had a facile Latinity. The extensive list of authors cited indicates that he had read widely, but digested little of what he read, in Patristic and Rabbinical literature. The purpose of the book is to discredit the claim of the Roman Church to the possession of supernatural gifts. The subjects dealt with are naturally the Roman sacraments and hagiology. The learned author arrives at the conclusion, on grounds which I have not had the patience to investigate, that the human exercise of miraculous powers ceased at the precise date, A.D. 430.

Of the writer, Doctor Makepeace, I can find little more information than is supplied in the History of Jesus College, written by John Sherman in the reign of Charles II. This work, composed in the fulsome Latin which was esteemed elegant in the seventeenth century, gives brief biographical notes of each of the Fellows from the date of the foundation of the College. There are various manuscript versions of the History, some ampler than others, and if you wish to read the original Latin, of which I subjoin a translation, you must search out the single copy which contains the full note of his life and work. It may be rendered:

"Matthew Makepeace, S.T.P., of the county of Northumberland, succeeded to a fellowship in 1565: a most learned investigator of theological matters (*rei theologicae indagator*), especially of the writings of the Fathers: a chastiser of the Pope (*Papomastix*): he illuminated by his knowledge the College and the University, most fearlessly attacking the unclean practices of the Babylonian harlot. He had one much-loved pupil, Marmaduke Dacre, firstborn son of the lord baron Dacre, of the county of Cumberland. The same having disappeared from the College in a fashion as yet unknown (*modo adhuc inscibili*) the old man, seized with a phrenetic malady, gradually declined (*contabuit*), often asserting that he was that same pupil whom he had lost. Dying at the age of sixty years, he was buried in the chapel, September 8th, 1604."

To the information given by Sherman I can only add the evidence of a blue flagstone — unhappily removed in the course of chapel restoration, in 1863 — which lay in the floor of the south transept. Its simple inscription was: "*Matthaeus Makepeace, S.T.P., decessit,* 1604".

With the evidence as to the date of the death of Dr Makepeace, furnished by Sherman and the old gravestone, it is difficult to reconcile a curious entry in the register of burials in All Saints' Parish Churchyard. The entry is dated April 13, 1654, and it runs: –

> "Matthew Makepeace, an oldman y^r lodged with ye widow Pearson in Jesus Lane, of ye age of about three score years and ten. He was burried in Poorman's Corner, by ye parish."

The date, the age of the deceased, the place of burial, the fact that this Makepeace was evidently a pauper and a stranger to Cambridge, all would seem to make it certain that he could not be the same man who is mentioned by Sherman. Nevertheless, I have my doubts, and the story which I have to unfold will explain the reason.

The story begins on August 16th, 1604, the very day on which the learned *Speculum* made its first appearance, bound and complete, on the table of Matthew Makepeace. The doctor's chamber was on an upper floor of the staircase at the western end of the chapel nave, and it overlooked what was then called Fair Yard, a plot of ground since annexed to the Master's garden. August 16th happened to be the last of the three days of Garlick Fair, the ancient fair which, since the days of King Stephen, had been associated with the Church of Saint Radegund, and took place under the chapel walls.

Matthew Makepeace was alone. It was Long Vacation, and his sole pupil, Marmaduke Dacre, who shared his chamber, had been allowed a day's outing. Heavy books of divinity lined the walls of the chamber, which had little of comfort about it and no elegance.

The doctor's high bed, with curtains of faded say, the pupil's truckle-bed, a hanging cupboard for clothes, a rough deal stand on which was set an ewer and basin of coarse earthenware, a chair, two stools and a large oaken table in the middle of the room — these were the doctor's principal household effects. There was but one window, of bottle-green glass, and its lattice was open to admit the air and sunlight of the August afternoon.

On the table lay the doctor's new book, brave in its stamped leather and gilded label: but it was unopened. It was the outcome of five and twenty years of incessant study, and the single offspring of Matthew's lucubration. And now that it was brought to birth he was in a mood to stifle it. It had been begun in the white heat of the controversies with Rome and Spain, and it lingered in parturition until the fire had burnt low, and the readers who should have applauded it were in their graves. Its author was not very sure that its contentions were true, and he was very sure that they were addressed to deaf ears. Had he gone out into the world he might have learnt what the world was interested in — what battles remained to fight, what causes were already finished. But Matthew's world consisted of books, and his books were out of date. Of recent political developments, of the growth of scientific knowledge, of the blossoming of a native literature he had no more knowledge than a child. The work which had been begun with enthusiasm had been completed in mechanical drudgery, and too late he was conscious of the fact.

How well he recollected the enthusiasms of 1579! How ardent his friends were that his immense learning should signalise itself in the great national strife with the powers of darkness! If he could only live his life again with the old enthusiasm and the added knowledge of a life that should combine learning and action! The boy, Dacre, blessed with genius, wealth, high birth and noble aspirations – how wide the horizon that opened before him! For Matthew Makepeace it rested only to be forgotten before he died.

It was a strange bird of passage that had dropped the seed from which Matthew's book grew. Alessandro Galiani was a medical doctor of Padua University when he came to Cambridge, and for a few months resided in Jesus College. Why he came nobody precisely knew; but he claimed to be a Protestant refugee, and he was certainly profoundly learned in many languages, as well as in medicine. He brought letters of introduction from the Chancellor, Lord Burleigh, and it was surmised that he was an agent of the Government, engaged to report on the University. But his talk and conduct were so equivocal that the suspicion presently arose that his Protestantism was simulated, and that he was a papal spy. The sentiments to which he gave expression were certainly Macchiavellian in the highest degree – intolerable to English ears. Wherefore his sojourn at Cambridge ended abruptly after a few months, and he passed away into the same mysterious spaces from which he had come. He was a man of extraordinary powers of observation and suggestion, and from a chance hint that he once let fall Makepeace got the idea of writing his book. It was Galiani who directed his attention to the Jewish and Arabic authors whom he consulted. But how little of the force and insight of the Italian entered into the completed book, Makepeace knew only too well.

So the book lay on the table and Matthew had no heart to open it. Through the window came sounds of merriment from the Fair Yard without. Regularly as August came round Makepeace had heard those sounds for forty years past, but until to-day he had regarded them only as a troublesome distraction, and closed his casement against them. To-day a profound lassitude made him draw his stool from the table, where lay the slighted volume, to the open window. His attention was especially drawn by a strident voice which came from near his chamber. Looking out on the Fair Yard he saw a platform of a few planks, mounted on casks, immediately beneath his window. On it a vagabond charlatan was loudly advertising to a group of gaping rustics the merits of a wonderful heal-all.

"Come buy, my masters, come buy," he cried. "Buy the infallible salve of the famous doctor Pinchbeck, the ointment that heals the ague, the rheum, the palsy, the serpigo. Let him that goes on one leg but buy, and with thrice laying on he shall go on two. Let him that goes with crutches buy, and he shall dance home in a coranto. One groat only for the learned doctor's ointment that shall quit you of the cramp, the gout, the quotidian and the tertian. An it rid you not in two days come again and Pinchbeck shall restore you fourfold."

From time to time an ague-ridden swain mounted the platform, haggled with the quack, reluctantly parted with his groat and departed, dubious of his purchase. On the whole, Dr Pinchbeck seemed to be doing a fair trade, when, late in the afternoon, an old man, bent double with rheumatism, raised a loud expostulation. He affirmed that he had purchased a box of the ointment on the first day of the fair, and had applied it thrice without the promised result.

He demanded the fourfold restitution of his money, and the mountebank stoutly resisted the claim. Angry cries arose from the bystanders, and it might have gone ill with the empiric, had not a diversion been effected by one of the crowd. This was a tall middle-aged man of somewhat dark complexion and foreign appearance, whose dress distinguished him as a gentleman and possibly a practiser of medicine. He stepped on the platform, spoke a few words to the ointment-vendor, and then, beckoning the old man to him, made him sit on a stool. He gazed fixedly for a few moments in the patient's eyes, made some mysterious motions of the hands before his face, whispered in his ear, and then, with a few more passes of his hands, bade him stand. The old fellow stood erect without effort; then, at the stranger's bidding, walked a few steps, and with a pleased and puzzled look descended to join his friends in the crowd. Loud applause greeted the wonderful cure, and patients crowded to receive the stranger's ministrations. The same operations in each case were attended with the same result. Never had there been seen such a wonder seen at the fair.

Most of all it wrought wonder in Matthew Makepeace. This unknown individual – was he possessed of those miraculous gifts of healing which Makepeace in 400 quarto pages had proved to be extinct? He would accost him and, if possible, learn from his lips whether what he had seen were the operation of nature or of the magic art. Descending in the majesty of his doctor's robes he mingled in the crowd, and mildly laid his hand on the stranger's arm. "Pardon, learned sir," said he, "the curiosity of a scholar — alas! Too ignorant of books and all unskilled in the manual acts of healing. I would fain question with you of these same cures that by chance I have witnessed from my chamber." The stranger was engaged in giving parting words of counsel to some of his patients. He turned at the touch of the doctor's hand, surveyed him up and down for a moment, and said, "Anon, Master Makepeace, anon: I will be with you presently."

Dr Makepeace started to hear his name and threw a sharp look on the speaker. No; he was a complete stranger, and his accent betrayed him as a foreigner. Dr Makepeace had certainly never seen him in his life before. He began to explain where his chamber was to be found.

"I know it," interrupted the stranger, "I know it. Bear with me for a moment and I will seek you there."

Makepeace was a little ruffled that the speaker, knowing his name, did not give him his academic title. "*Doctor* Makepeace," he said; "ask for *Doctor* Makepeace."

"Surely, surely," replied the stranger carelessly: "yet *Master* Makepeace, methinks, served you then."

More than ever perplexed the doctor sought his room. Only a few minutes had passed when he heard his visitor mounting with no faltering step to his door, and Makepeace opened to him before he knocked. The stranger glanced rapidly round. He seemed to find something familiar in each article of furniture. He ran his eye, with a look of some amused contempt, over the array of worn volumes that lined the walls. "Old books, doctor Makepeace," he said, "old books. I think you have not changed one these thirty years."

"Old books are old friends," said the doctor with a touch of resentment at his tone: "I would not change them."

"Old friends die, doctor," observed the stranger, "they die, and then we have no use for them but to bury them."

"Sir," said the doctor with a quick reminiscence of his wasted studies, "I *have* buried my friends: but I love them still. But," he went on, "it is not of old notions that I have to speak with you. You have shown me this afternoon something newer and," he added sadly, "it may be, something better than all that old books tell. I ask you to impart to me no secret that might hurt you by the telling. Until now I have maintained that nothing exists in this present world that is not of natural course. If it be an honest mystery that you exercise, tell me, the humblest and poorest of scholars, whether it be the miraculous working of God's power in human hands or simply the exercise of human art."

The stranger seated himself, uninvited, in the doctor's chair, and the doctor took a stool. "Everything," said the stranger, "is miracle to him who does not know."

"Great heavens," cried Makepeace, "that is the beginning of my quotation from the learned Theodorus Gazophylacius. I never heard of the great Gazophylacius until Galiani told me of him: nobody that I know had heard of him. A marvellous scholar, truly, was Gazophylacius, but a pagan at heart, albeit a Byzantine Christian – and sadly drowned in superstition. Shall I show you the passage in the original Greek?" And he feverishly turned the pages of the *Speculum* to find it.

The Burden of Dead Books

Chapel Doorway in Master's Garden.

"You may spare yourself that trouble," said the stranger composedly. "Shall I finish the quotation? Shall I write it for you?" And he unceremoniously tore a corner from one of the immaculate leaves, took a quill and wrote. "There," said he, "there, I have written in Greek what follows in your quotation, and I have added my name that you may remember the writer." The doctor took it and read the delicate Greek characters: "Demetrius Commagenus. All things are possible to him who knows and wills with earnestness."

Makepeace was stupified. "Commagenus," he said: "that is a Greek name, I take it. And yet I would have sworn that the handwriting was Galiani's, and Galiani was an Italian. Besides, Galiani is dead, or he is sixty years old, less or more, by now: and you – I cannot think that you are past forty."

Indifferently the self-styled Commagenus replied: "Galiani or Commagenus – what matters? What I wrote then I write now; and always I am your humble servant and the poor scholar who drew wisdom from the lips of the divine Gazophylacius."

"We talk in dreams," said Matthew: "Galiani told me – you told me, if you are he – that Gazophylacius died in Rome, ten years after the Turks entered Constantinople: and that was a hundred and fifty years ago."

"Yes," answered Commagenus, "he died – the more is the pity; for he might have lived, had he chosen to use his own wisdom. Instead of that he imparted it on his death-bed to me. What care had he to live, an outcast in strange lands? But this world lost its wisest man; for I am no Gazophylacius. Only I am always learning."

"Why, this is as strange a maze as ever man trod," cried Makepeace. "You tell me that your master died a hundred and forty years ago, and that you, Galiani, were with him at the time."

"Not Galiani, but Commagenus," said the stranger in complacent amusement at the doctor's bewilderment: "that was my name then. I was a youth, twenty years old, when I first came to Constantinople from the country which gave me my name – three years before the siege. There I became the favourite pupil of the great student of natural and medical science, Theodorus Gazophylacius."

"Why, that makes you a hundred and seventy years old," feebly remonstrated Makepeace. "Are you then the Wandering Jew?"

"Doctor, I am shocked," said Commagenus. "Are such fables the stuff of which the *Speculum* is made? I tell you there is nothing in this world that is not natural. That was my master's constant teaching: also that to know and to will makes man master of nature. That much I learnt from him while he taught at Constantinople, and it was in my noviciate that I gathered from him the art to work such simple cures as you saw this afternoon. To prolong mere existence by keeping disease at bay – that he esteemed a vulgar art. To live long and die old, feeble and foolish – what gain is that to the man or his fellow-men? To live always, always to be young, always eager, always to be growing in wisdom and power – that was the secret for which he spent a lifetime's search, and with his dying breath he told me that he had sought it in vain. Death, the last disease, is incurable: there is a stronger will than man's. But he told me of a door of escape. In his last moments he was possessed with a dread that his discovery would perish in the general eclipse of learning which he foresaw as the result of the disappearance of the Byzantine schools, and, with solemn admonition as to its use, he imparted it to me. Death, the mere accident of the flesh, is transferable with the flesh. With will and knowledge, the spirit – all that you call character, intelligence, consciousness, memory – may pass from form to form, unchanged in the transition and always capable of growth and ripening. Alas, that I have not made better use of my master's prescriptions! But it has been my evil fate. Another might do better."

"These are heathen imaginings – snares and delusions of Satan," cried Makepeace. "What talk is this of tampering with the divine in us? Man, are you a Christian?"

"I am what I am," replied Commagenus: "but that this is waking fact and no delusion my history shall show you. After my beloved master's death I set up in medical practice in a certain city of Dalmatia. The fame of my unusual healing powers spread in all the neighbourhood. Unfortunately it reached the ears of the bishop of the diocese. He was a sincere, well-meaning man, kind in all his relations with the laity of his diocese, but a trifle superstitious. He concluded that I was a necromancer and condemned me to be burnt alive. Until the moment when I found myself in a dungeon and on the eve of execution I had never thought to avail myself of the secret communicated to me by my master, and had even questioned its efficacy. The prospect of burning was so extremely repugnant to my feelings that I resolved to make practical trial of it. Shall I show you how it is done? No, you need not shrink from me. I have no wish to pass into simple old Matthew Makepeace. I can do better. Be assured that the will goes not with the act."

Commagenus rose and fastened his gaze on Matthew. As he did so it seemed to the doctor that he grew and grew to a bulk and stature ineffable and dim. But that, he reasoned with himself, was an illusion of the sense, and for the moments when the fascinating glare was fixed on him he retained his consciousness. Slowly, deliberately, that Matthew might follow every movement in succession, he moved his hands and arms in gyrations and waves more intricate than any Matthew had witnessed when the Greek stood on the mountebank's platform that afternoon. Then he stooped over the table, and with extraordinary distinctness of articulation whispered in his ear one word. What that word was I do not know. Matthew Makepeace remembered it once, and forgot it for all the years that he lived afterwards.

The Greek took up his tale again. "My excellent master had informed me that, whether the subject were waking or asleep, the will and the word had equal effect. My gaoler slept in the condemned cell with me and the occasion seemed to me a particularly happy one for testing the accuracy of my master's conclusions. Though I did not doubt the intensity of my will, in prospect of such an undesirable event as being burnt alive, I confess that I was surprised and more than gratified by the issue of the experiment. I had the satisfaction of leading my gaoler to the stake on the following morning."

"What," cried Makepeace: "do you tell me that the man was burnt? True," he added, as a mitigating consideration suggested itself to his bewildered brain, "he was a papist. But, after all, what were you?"

Commagenus answered with the resignation of a parent satisfying an inquisitive child. "Yes, Matthew Makepeace, when your raiment is past your own use you make a gift of it to some humble dependent. When *he* has worn it threadbare, what happens? It is burnt. You do not burn it: I did not burn him. Besides, this common man in ages to come will be held in reverence – in another name, I admit – as a martyr to medical science. Nevertheless I was little pleased, as you may think, with the integument which my brutal gaoler had left me. In my new and humble sphere of life I had few opportunities of self-improvement, and, taking the first that offered, I installed myself in the person of a Dominican friar. I am disposed to doubt whether I really bettered myself by my change of profession. I found that it required much ingenuity to sustain the part of crass ignorance which was associated with my new character, and the man's companions were deplorable people. An accident, which had nearly proved fatal, relieved me of the disagreeable situation. In the course of my professional duties I was directed to take ship for Spain, where the Dominican order had an especial interest in the Office of the Holy Inquisition. On the voyage we fell in with a vessel belonging to a respectable merchant of Marseilles. The merchant, who was likewise the ship's captain, was in the habit, when occasion offered, of diversifying the routine of commerce by piratical enterprise. With his crew he boarded and took possession of our vessel, informing us that we were his prisoners. As he had a reputation for probity to sustain at Marseilles, he judged it prudent to throw the whole of the crew and passengers of our vessel into the waves. However, learning that there was a clergyman on board, he seized the opportunity of making confession first and receiving plenary absolution from him of an outstanding balance of prior delinquencies. It was natural to avail myself of the opportunity for transferring myself into his person. It was pleasant to see him flounder in the sea with the rest, and I returned – if that is the right word – to Marseilles, in circumstances sufficiently ample to warrant retirement from a profession the ambiguous character of which offended my moral sense. But my experiences in the three careers of life which my destiny had recently forced upon me gave me an indelible prejudice against the Western Church. On the whole I am a Protestant.

"I need not detain you with my subsequent transmigrations. The merchant was elderly and so oppressively respectable that I was glad to exchange into the superior rank of a French marquisate. Since then, from Trebizond to Tarifa, I have studied men and manners in many capacities. Perhaps the time which was pleasantest to me, as a man of science, was spent in Peru with Pizarro, whom I attended as a captain of cavalry. But a fatal wound, inflicted by a poisoned arrow, compelled my return to Spain in the office of a ship's boatswain. After all my wanderings my conscience reproached me with my culpable neglect of the art in whose elements I had been grounded by the ever-revered Gazophylacius. I resumed the medical studies which I was convinced were best suited to my bent and upbringing, by adopting the features and the status of a freshman in the University of Padua. As the freshman, under no possible circumstances, could have passed his examinations you will see that I conferred on him no small obligation by the assistance which I rendered. In my first year I obtained advancement to the person and professorial chair of Galiani. I am grieved to tell you that I left him seriously unwell at Salerno, ten years ago; and his decease, which followed almost immediately after, proved to me how wise had been my course in transferring myself into the healthy frame of the brother professor who attended him in the earlier phases of his malady. Come, doctor, you have let me chatter on with these tiresome details till I see you are three parts asleep."

"Asleep!" roared Makepeace, who had been filled with rage, disgust and hatred by the shameless recital. "Asleep! Wretch, thief, assassin, defiler of the sanctuary of man! Begone, skirr, fly! Would that I could crush your basilisk head on the floor as I stand! But stay. I will fetch the University bedel. He shall clap you in the lowest hold of the Castle Gaol."

"Marry, good words, master doctor," said the imperturbable stranger. "Your bedel, possibly, is a family man; and conscience forbids that, except in the last resort, I should lay a father of a family in a dungeon for crimes that, you are pleased to assert, are of my doing: and, except that I do not propose myself for the office of bedel, it were an easy thing for me to do so. Getting old is a sad affair, sadder even than dying. I think that you are sixty, and I don't think that just now you are quite in your best health. Has the world gone very well with you? In five years, ten years, will it go better? You have written a silly book that nobody will read, and you are ashamed of it. You have wasted your years of manhood in twisting ropes of sand. And the solitude, Matthew! My heart bleeds to think what your solitude will be. What friend have you to smooth the downhill course? Who cares for the friend of dead books? Altogether, you have very little use now for Matthew Makepeace. Who is it that should sleep in yonder bed?" He asked, pointing to the truckle used by Marmaduke Dacre. "Is he young? Is he comely? Has he friends to love him and be loved? Is he of a quick spirit and high hope. Matthew Makepeace, you know the acts and the word. The door lies open to you. Take wisdom, and be young."

"The door lies open to *you*," shouted Makepeace, throwing it open as he spoke. "Pass out of it, and avoid the chamber of a Christian man: and the foul fiend fly away with you and your abominable suggestions!"

"Doctor Makepeace, I wish you a very good evening," said his visitor.

The night was far advanced, and Matthew Makepeace had no mind for bed. A dim rush candle, set on a stool in a corner of the apartment, cast flickering shadows on the walls and floor. In an opposite dark corner his pupil slept. But for the dread of awaking him, Makepeace would have paced the room in his perplexity. As it was, he sat bent double on the stool by the window.

One thing was clear enough. If what he had seen and heard was not a fiction or the delusion of his senses, the *Speculum* was a colossal stupidity. Even if the rejuvenations of Commagenus were as much in the course of nature as he affirmed them to be, did they not warrant the Pope's most arrogant pretensions? But it was with himself that he was most concerned. Was it not the fact that, as Commagenus had declared, his life had been most miserably wasted? And the mistake was past repair. If only his youth had known! And his mind went back to a short, happy time, just after he had taken his degree, when he had served as chaplain in his far-away northern country, at the ancestral castle of the Dacres. His pupil then had been the present Lord, Marmaduke's father; and the pupil had had so much to teach his master about hawks and horses and hounds that the master had little leisure to repay it in Greek and Latin. Those were happy days when they had roamed the Cumbrian fells together. And now this Lord Dacre was great in the councils of his sovereign, the wise and respected ruler of a barony that was almost a kingdom in itself. And in his trusting confidence he had committed his son to the care of his old master at Cambridge; and that son in course of years would naturally succeed to his father's station.

Had Commagenus indeed sat in that chamber, only a few hours since, and unfolded to him the secret of perpetual youth? Yes: there was the evidence of the written scrap lying on the open page of the *Speculum*. True, Commagenus had made a detestable use of his wonderful power. But with Makepeace it would be different. He was conscious of his sobriety and virtue, and there were the noble traditions of the house of Dacre to keep him in the right way. He had abilities, if only he had youth and opportunity to use them, and the experience of sixty years was a better guarantee for their proper employment than any that a callow youth could offer. Clearer, louder than the voices of conscience or calculation there came back to him, like the drumming burden of an iterated song, the words "The door is open. Be young." Was it fancy that a door seemed to open in the dark book-press opposite, and that through it he looked out on a sunny haze enveloping blue hills and waters and the towers of Dacre Castle? And cool breaths from heathery heights took up the refrain, and whispered to him "Be young".

Matthew Makepeace crept quietly to the dark corner where his pupil lay. His will was intense as he had never known it before. He took care that his shadow should not fall on the sleeper's face and arouse him. He made the wonderful passes – with what extraordinary clearness they were printed on his recollection! He stooped and whispered in his pupil's ear the mysterious word.

If Matthew had expected a flash of lightning, the apparition of the Evil One, the jubilations of triumphant fiends on the success of his experiment, he was agreeably disappointed. Nothing of the kind happened. Only in the dim light of the candle he saw a grey shadow of weary age steal over his pupil's face, and he felt the vigour and vitality of youth invade his own limbs as with the intoxication of wine. Then the wick suddenly flickered in the candle-socket and went out. He heard Marmaduke turn over in his bed with an uneasy sigh.

Then Makepeace woke to reason and a horrible dread. He dared not relight the candle for fear of rousing the sleeper. In the dark, before he was discovered, he must repeat the process which should restore each to his own person. In the dark, as nearly as he could, he went through the magical passes, and with extraordinary vehemence he willed himself back into Matthew Makepeace. But the word! Great heavens! It had passed from him as suddenly and completely as the light of the extinguished candle. In vain he racked his memory of every language, living or dead: of that he felt sure, and he was sure of nothing else. For an hour, by his pupil's bedside, he tore his hair in desperate efforts to recall it. For an hour he alternately cursed Commagenus and prayed that he might return before day to give him the forgotten word. Then the grey morning light began to creep through the casement, and the birds woke and sang.

There could be no shadow of doubt about it. There lay Matthew Makepeace before him, and the old man was drowsily stirring his limbs as the light broadened into day. And young Dacre, in a doctor's gown, was looking down upon him, tortured with horrible thoughts. One thing was certain. He could never pass himself off as Marmaduke. Conscience, gratitude, affection forbade it. Besides, the thing was impossible. He, the torpid pedant, could never play the part of the young and chivalrous heir of the Dacres: and there would be Marmaduke to convict the imposture. Before his pupil woke, before the discovery was made, he must disappear from Cambridge. Quietly and in haste he took down his pupil's clothes from the closet where they hung, and exchanged for them his doctor's robes. Then he descended his stairs and stepped out into the cool shadows of the August morning. The porter was just opening the gate. He nodded familiarly to young Dacre as he passed. That was the last which any soul in Jesus College saw of Matthew Makepeace.

Unless, indeed, it were that same Matthew Makepeace who, with the homing instinct of a dying animal, crept back to Cambridge in poverty and wretchedness, and died in widow Pearson's house in 1654. In any case the flagstone in the chapel transept told a lie: it was Marmaduke Dacre that lay beneath it.

One thing further I have to mention. When I first took down the *Speculum* from its shelf in the college library I found it in the same virgin condition in which it had lain on the table of Matthew Makepeace on that fatal afternoon in August 1604. No living soul had disturbed its repose for over 300 years. It was evidently the same copy: perhaps no other was ever issued. As I turned its pages a scrap of paper fluttered to the floor. It had been torn from the bottom corner of pages 273–4. On it was written in minute Greek letters an inscription which I translate:

"Demetrius Commagenus. All things are possible to him who knows and wills with earnestness."

Thankfull Thomas

 PASSAGE IN THE lately edited *Diary of George Evans*, 1649–1658, has called my attention to a singular and, I believe, unrecorded episode in the history of Jesus College.

With Mr Evans himself the story is not concerned. It is sufficient to say that he was appointed to a fellowship at Jesus in 1650 by the Committee for Reforming the Universities, in place of an expelled Presbyterian. He was, as his name suggests, a Welshman, of the county of Radnor, and, of course, an Independent. He vacated his fellowship, on his marriage, in 1654, and retired to the living of Marston Monceux, co. Salop. He held the incumbency until his death, in 1672, having conformed at the Restoration.

The portion of his diary which has awaked my interest relates to the date June 11, 1652. For its explanation it is necessary to state that ten years previously, just before the outbreak of the Civil War, the College had taken a quantity of its plate from the Treasury and delivered it to a certain Mr John Poley, by him to be conveyed to His Majesty, who was then in Nottingham. As the whole society was under menace of expulsion before the end of 1642, they took the precaution, before quitting the College, of concealing the rest of the plate, as well as the chapel organ. This organ had been introduced in 1634 by the Master, Richard Sterne, who was Archbishop Laud's chaplain, and had actively promoted his plans for the re-organisation of church ritual in the University. It was a small chamber instrument, easily transportable. When the new society, consisting of Presbyterians introduced by the Earl of Manchester, entered the College in January, 1643, they noted in the Treasury Book that they could only discover three pieces of plate. Entries in the Bursar's Book in the year 1652 record that the rest of the plate was discovered in that year, and at a rather later date the organ was brought to light.

Some further notes respecting the Chapel in Commonwealth days will serve to explain certain points in the history which I have been able to unravel. The older of the two existing bells in the tower was cast by Christopher Gray in 1659. It took the place of another which was of pre-Reformation date and had probably served the Nunnery of Saint Radegund. This was a heavy tenor bell, and had apparently belonged to a set of four, named after the evangelists. It bore the emblem of Saint Mark, a lion, and the inscription in ancient lettering —

Celorvm Marce resonet tvvs ympnvs in Arce

This bell, for many years previous to 1652, had been disused owing to the weakness of its frame and of the supporting floor.

The passage, above referred to, in George Evans' diary runs as follows:

"June 11 [1652]. Present ye Master, Mr Woodcocke and Mr Machin, fellows, with Mr Thomas Buck, Thankfull Thomas and Robert Hitchcock digging, we digged up ye treasury plate hidd in ye Masters orchard. In all were seventeen peeces (then follows a list). Searched till prayers. But Quaerendm whether there be not yit other peeces and ye treasure hidd by ye former societie. Thomas saith Mr Germyn cld avouch for more."

On reading this extract, the name – for such it seemed to be – Thankfull Thomas, at once arrested my attention. It reminded me of a partially obliterated inscription on a flat gravestone which lies at the crossing of the transepts, close to the south-west pier of the tower – that one which is distinguished from the other piers by a dog-tooth moulding. The letters are so worn by treading that they can only be distinguished in certain lights, and indeed have altogether disappeared on the side of the stone which is furthest from the pier-base. What remains is to be read:-

nkfull

mas

Followed by a date of which the figures *652* are legible.

I have searched the Register of the College for such a name, but, though it is complete for the years preceding 1652, I have been unable to find it. But in the College Order Book I have found, among other appointments of the year 1650, an entry, "Thomas constitutus est Custos Templi." From which it would seem that Thomas was the surname of the Independent official corresponding to a verger or chapel-clerk. It is singular that he should have been buried, among Masters and Fellows, in such a conspicuous place in the Chapel.

The discovery of the plate in the Master's orchard – brought about through the agency of Mr Thomas Buck, of Catharine Hall, who was one of the Esquire Bedells – was matter for disappointment as much as congratulation to the Master and Fellows. They had a convinced belief that a much larger quantity of treasure remained concealed in some quarter of the College, and, as the passage in the diary shows, Thankfull Thomas suggested that Mr Germyn probably knew something of the matter. Of him it is necessary to say a few words.

Gervase Germyn, of the county of Huntingdon, was admitted to the College in 1621, and in 1652 must have been a man of middle age. He was a Master of Arts, unmarried, and resided in Cambridge. He was not one of the expelled Fellows. He had acted as organist and choir-master in the mastership of Richard Sterne, and was passionately devoted to church music. After the removal of the organ and the installation of the new Master and Fellows, in 1643, his connection with the College ceased. He was miserably poor and supported himself by teaching music. His small, spare figure was ordinarily dressed in a thread-bare garb of semi-clerical appearance, and he had a quaintness of manner and speech which induced the belief that he was not of ordinary sanity.

Thankfull Thomas particularly disliked him. Gervase had a tone of superiority in addressing him which was the more galling because what he said was only remotely intelligible to the sexton; and he had a disagreeable habit of meddling with what he considered to be the duties and prerogatives of his office. Germyn must have possessed a key to the Chapel, for he was constantly presenting himself there at unexpected times, often late in the evening. He had a distracting habit of roaming about the building, and, as Thomas thought, spying on his actions from unseen quarters. Thomas had seen him looking down on him from the Nuns' gallery in the north transept, or high up in the tower arcade.

Thomas took note of these circumstances and kept his knowledge to himself. His cupidity was aroused by the thought of the hidden treasure, and he was perfectly convinced that the clue to its discovery lay with Germyn. As it was useless to question him directly he resorted to a system of counter-espial.

His attention was particularly drawn to the Chapel tower, where he had more than once detected Germyn's presence. The arcaded storey beneath the belfry is reached by a dark, winding stair in the wall at the north-east angle of the north transept. The staircase emerges, at a considerable height, on a Norman gallery, which, at the time of which I am speaking, was not protected on the transept side by a railing. Thomas was a timid man, and he made this alarming passage

Norman Gallery, North Transept.

clutching each pillar as he passed it. Then another stair in the tower pier led up to the arcaded gallery, and there the inner communication stopped. A door in the north arcade opened on the roof of the transept, from which a dizzy ladder ascended to the belfry window. The ladder gave Thomas pause. It was old, weather-worn and crazy, and, unless by the light figure of Germyn, had perhaps never been scaled for a generation. The silent belfry above, encompassed by wheeling jackdaws, was a terror to his weak nerves. Even from the floor below he could see the gaping rottenness of its rafters: so he let it alone.

Secure on the Chapel floor he began his researches. In his vacant moments he roamed about chancel, transepts and nave, beating the walls and trampling the flags, if perchance he might light on some recess wherein the treasure was contained. At first his curiosity was excited by certain crosses graved on the nave floor. He did not know that they marked the processional path of the Saint Radegund nuns. But he could detect no sound of hollowness beneath them. Finally, he fastened his mind on a large, unmarked stone, next the south-west pier of the tower. Here, and in no other part of the Chapel, there was distinct evidence that a vault of some kind existed. Above it the disused bell-rope was attached to the pier.

Often, when the Chapel was closed after service hours, he scrutinised this stone. It had no mark of recent disturbance, but in ten years it was likely that any such indication had been obliterated. One summer evening in 1652 he was so engaged, and kneeling on the stone, when he was startled by the sudden falling of a shadow. He sprang to his feet and beheld Gervase Germyn.

"Good evening, friend," said Germyn. "You work late. I was visiting some old friends that lie under the stones here, having a word with him or him that I have known, a remembered jest with one, a snatch of old song with another — who knows what? And here are you at the like business. And who, pray, is your friend?"

"Master Germyn," replied Thomas stiffly, "an idle man may talk to dead men, if he will: a sexton has other business with them. How often am I to bid you not to meddle in my affairs?"

"You are very right," said Germyn, "and now I perceive this is no man's grave — yet. Perhaps the sexton is looking to make it one. And which, pray, of my friends, the new Fellows, has gone to his audit? Or is it to be mine, perhaps, or thine: and I think it be thine indeed, for I find thee lying on it. But you don't know the Prince of Denmark: else I should ask you the clown's riddle, 'What is he that builds stronger than either the mason, the shipwright, or the carpenter?' It is a pretty riddle to ask within walls that are five hundred years old."

"I make no graves," answered Thomas, "and I have no time or patience for your riddles. I only ask you to begone."

"Is the trade then so slack, friend Thomas, and is there none to give the sexton employment? — none of all that dig for death as for hid treasure, and some, perhaps, who dig for treasure and find death."

Thomas was startled at the hint that his purpose was detected. He looked dubiously on the speaker, and the thought dawned on him that perhaps Germyn was offering himself as a confederate. "Treasure," he said slowly; "yes, if you talk of treasure there is more sense in you than I thought. I don't know but what we might find it together; and a poor man, such as you, might have his fair share, and none be the wiser."

"You are wholly mistaken," said Germyn, "if you think that I know anything of the treasure that you are looking for: and, if I knew, God forbid that I should rob the dead of their trust. No, let them keep it until the day of restitution, when their friends claim it of them. You are a bold man, Thomas, to think of the dead as if they had no sense of what happens to-day. For my part, though we talk as old friends, I have a dreadful awe of them: they can do so much, and I can't hurt them, if I would. It is a marvel to me that you can walk and work at such an hour in a place that is so full of voices and presences. A holy man you should be! Do you know how Goodman Deane, the last man who held your office, died?"

"They tell me he died distracted. But I don't trouble myself with fancies."

"It was in August, two years since. What had he seen? What had he heard? They say that in his wanderings he often repeated 'I should have rung, I should have rung.' And I think I see his meaning. It is an old belief – God knows what of truth there is in it – that at the ringing of the church bell the congregations of the dead break up and give place to the living. Poor Deane! Mark could not speak for him: he has been dumb these twenty years, though one day, please God, he will speak again for his friends – of whom you are not one. And there is another old fancy that belongs to this church, and perhaps had something to do with Deane's matter. It used to be told among the old society, that are scattered or dead now, that the festival of the Name of Jesus was a great day with the old dead folk. Each year at midnight on that day, which is the seventh of August, they assemble — men or women, I know not which — here in the church to observe the hours of Lauds. It was said that you could hear them trooping down from their chambers outside by a stair that does not exist, and they came through the church wall by a door that is unseen. Then, each in order, they rank themselves on the crosses that mark the pavement, and go round the church in darkness, for they need no lights. Their singing has been often heard, but I do not know that living eye has seen their procession, unless it were Deane's, and, it seems, he did not live long after."

"It is a curious fancy, truly," said Thomas, "if one could credit it. But I don't know why you tell it me, as I never visit the church after nightfall. And little as I believe your tale, I believe you less when you tell me that you know nothing of this treasure. But I spoke of it at a venture, and it is none of my business. So I leave you to your ghosts."

Thankfull Thomas was not courageous, but his fears were not of a sentimental order. He was more than ever convinced that Germyn knew the secret of the hidden treasure, and that his story was a device to prevent him from continuing his search for it; and he had made up his mind that it lay under the stone where Germyn had interrupted him. At night he would be secure from his interference, and would have time to lift the stone and replace it in such a manner

Thankfull Thomas

South West Pier of Tower.

as to leave no trace of its disturbance. And as the date which Germyn had mentioned had passed out of his mind, it so happened that August 7 was the night which he chose for his enterprise.

It was past eleven when he entered the church with lantern and tools. The stone was heavy, and it took a considerable time to dislodge and lift it. Beneath it he saw a vault, some five feet deep. He lowered his lamp into it. Great was his disappointment to find it blankly empty. He had so fastened his expectations on this particular spot that hardly yet could he think himself mistaken. He let himself down into the vault that he might explore for some recess in its walls or floor.

He was still groping in semi-gloom when, above his head, he caught the sound of quiet treading, and then a waft of strange music. He was too unskilled to tell what the instrument might be, but the sound of it was soft and pleasant. It rose, and died away, and rose again in fitful strains. Then it went on in a continuous melody and was taken up by a voice particularly sweet and clear – so clear that the words were plainly distinguishable. "When the Lord turned again the captivity of Sion then were we like unto them that dream."

Thomas listened in amazement till the psalm ended and silence returned. Then he heard the shuffling of descending steps, and with a sudden horror he remembered the story of the dead men's staircase and the phantom procession. He heard a door softly open in the dark transept, and he sprang wildly to the bell-rope above his head. One frightful clang: Mark spoke again after twenty years of silence: a rumble and a roar: the heavy bell splintered itself on the floor beneath, and Thankfull Thomas, in a pool of blood, lay in the grave of his own making.

In a corner of the belfry, where the floor was not broken by the falling bell, they discovered the organ, which had been hidden there since 1642.

The Restoration brought back a few survivors of the expelled Society of 1642, and with them Gervase Germyn. But in 1664 I find that George Loosemore was master of the College choristers, and Germyn was dead. At what precise date he died I cannot say. But one thing is known. The Chapel, after long neglect and misappropriation, was repaired, decorated and restored to Anglican usage about the year 1663. The reconciliation of the Church was marked by a choral service, and Germyn occupied his old seat at the organ. Among the psalms chosen for the service was the 126th, *In convertendo captivitatem Sion*. The singers had reached the last verse – "He that now goeth on his way weeping and beareth forth good seed: shall doubtless come again with joy and bring his sheaves with him." There the organ accompaniment faltered, failed, died, and left the choir to chant the *Gloria* unassisted. The grey head of Gervase Germyn lay on the keyboard, and the College had to seek a new organist.

The Palladium

N AN UNSPECIFIED morning in the year 1026, in the reign of Cnut, king, of happy memory, Aethelstan, abbat of Ramsey, delivered to the monks of his Benedictine household, in chapter assembled, an address which had notable consequences.

The reverend father took as the text of his discourse the verse, *in libro Regum tertio*, which in our Authorised Version is expressed – Know ye not that Ramoth in Gilead is ours, and we be still, and take it not out of the hand of the King of Syria?

With the ghostly lessons to be drawn from this passage we need not concern ourselves: indeed they were but lightly touched upon by the abbat. He turned almost directly to practical matters.

He dwelt feelingly on the palpable evidences of the poverty of their household – the bell-tower of their church, which had fallen in sudden ruin, and which the means of their household did not permit them to rebuild: the indecent sordidness of their chapter-house, within whose mud-built walls they were then assembled: the meagreness of the monastic diet, of which his brethren were the last to complain, but which reflected unfavourably on the coldness of Christian charity in the laity of the neighbourhood. And incidentally he contrasted these conditions with the splendour of the new temple, adorned with goodly stones and gifts, which their beloved friends at Ely had erected since the Danish wars had ended: the ephods of purple and scarlet affected by the ministers in Saint Etheldreda's church: and the proverbial magnificence of Ely feasts.

He asked himself the cause of this contrast, and with humility he confessed that it lay in the remissness of himself and his venerable predecessors in the abbatial seat of Ramsey. He commended to the attention of his hearers a text, *in fine libri Josue*, in which it was recorded that the children of Israel had brought up the bones of Joseph with them from Egypt, and that the said bones had become the inheritance of the children of Joseph: and he enlarged on the advantages, pecuniary as well as spiritual, which undoubtedly rewarded those children.

What had Ramsey done to emulate an example so worthy? Nothing, or next to nothing. At a cost relatively small they had, indeed, procured from an ignorant rustic, who had dug them up at the town of Slepe, some bones which competent authority declared to be those of the Persian bishop, Saint Yvo. But, whether or not the cause lay in some lack of orthodoxy in this oriental prelate, it must be confessed that his remains had not been so miraculously effectual in procuring the liberality of the laity as had been anticipated. He ventured to suggest that the relics of a local saint might be more successful. He casually drew their attention in this matter to the example of the holy brethren of Ely. Not content with their heritage of the bones of Saint Etheldreda and the virgins, her relatives, they had recently forcibly detained and appropriated a consignment of the remains of Aednoth, bishop of Dorchester, addressed to Ramsey Abbey and belonging of right to it. While he did not defend the methods of their Ely brethren, he must applaud their conspicuous and practical piety.

The abbat deplored the circumstance that the vicinity of their abbey had produced no saint of such eminent merits as to transmit to his remains the powers that should evoke the faith and the funds so necessary to their present needs. As an illustration of the spirit which he would like to find among his own brethren he again invited their attention to the religious activity of their friends of Ely, who had despatched a naval and military force as far as Dereham, in Norfolk, and with tumult of war had abstracted from the church there the shrine and body of Saint Withburga, virgin. In fact the pious solicitude of their friends had sometimes carried them to lengths which, making the widest allowance for the purity of their motives, the abbat could not regard as otherwise than regrettable. In the recent Danish troubles the brethren of Saint Alban's had committed to the safe keeping of the Ely monks the shrine containing the relics of the great Protomartyr of Britain. At the restoration of peace the Ely people had, indeed, returned the chest, but they afterwards maintained that they had substituted in it the remains of a less sacred person and had kept Saint Alban in their church. The Saint Alban's brotherhood on their part asserted that, from a conscientious regard for the sanctity of their trust, they had thought well not to part with the veritable person of their tutelar saint, but to employ the pardonable strategem of enclosing an inferior substitute in the shrine despatched to Ely. But the point in dispute was immaterial, inasmuch as the Ely relics, to whomsoever they had originally appertained, had contributed largely to the prosperity of that household, while the event proved that the proprietary interests of Saint Alban's had been in no degree prejudiced. Blind Isaac bestowed the same blessing of earth's fatness on supplanting Jacob and on first-born Esau. Charity and prudence alike dictated that, in the hearing of the giver, there should be no contention between brotherly households about a birth-right which, for all practical uses, each of them possessed in its integrity.

To what did the abbat's observations tend? At the obscure church of Soham, Cambs., unworthy receptacle of so divine a treasure, rested what had been mortal of Saint Felix, bishop and evangelist of the East Angles. The bishop of the diocese in which Ramsey was situated, at the abbat's instance, had procured royal letters patent authorising the Ramsey monks to transfer the sacred remains to their conventual church. Far be it from him to suggest such violent courses as had, in some measure, clouded the effulgent zeal of their Ely neighbours. The Soham folk, if properly approached, would, no doubt, show themselves compliant to the King's will, and would be eager to collaborate in a work so happily inspired. He requested the chapter to express its views as to the proper methods of attaining their pious object of putting the bell-tower in a condition of permanent stability.

Prior Alfwin rose and, protesting veneration for his Superior, ventured to offer some remarks which, he trusted, would not be regarded as derogating from the respect due to the abbatial chair. Fraternal affection had, in his opinion, betrayed the Lord Abbat into an estimate of the character of the Ely people which was not warranted by the facts. The prior regarded them as sons of Belial. By what instinct of the Devil the holy father, Saint Aethelwold, had induced King Edgar to endow their monastery with wealth so disproportioned to their merits it was not for him to surmise. Among the estates so granted was the manor of Soham. There could be no doubt that, if they got wind of the proposed translation of their saint, the Soham men would fight. It would ill become their sacred calling to employ the carnal weapons to which the Ely brigands had resorted. "Let us rather," said the prior, "attain our ends by friendly gifts and such arts as are permissible to our peaceful profession — wine, for instance, or beer." The rest of the prior's observations were directed to a discussion of the properties of poppy, mandragora and other soporific herbs.

After general discussion it was agreed that a letter should be despatched to the reeve of Soham, announcing the intention of the abbat and prior of paying their observance at the shrine of Saint Felix on an appointed day: that the abbey boat-carls should be in attendance to convey those officials thither from Erith hithe in the household barge: and that the cellarer should make such provision for the entertainment of the residents in Soham as might seem to his prudence expedient.

Brother Brihtmer, lately professed, added the observation that he knew a man or two — servants or tenants of the Abbey — Oswi, the miller, for instance, who carried off the ram for wrestling at Bury fair. With a few such at Erith he thought that he might be trusted to discuss the situation with the Ely men, if they got so far. He would also provide ten stout carls to row the barge from Erith to Soham and to undertake what else might be required of them at the latter place.

It was a notable day in the annals of the little town of Soham when the Ramsey barge, propelled by ten rowers, five a side, clad in the abbey uniform of bare arms and legs and a loose gown of green falding, was sighted on the far side of Soham mere. Quite a considerable throng of the principal inhabitants watched it from the wooden jetty, to which were moored the cobbles of the Soham fishermen. The reeve, in a murrey coat and blue hood, was an important figure in the group, and was accompanied by a select party of the leading sokemen. The local clergy were in attendance with a hastily improvised band of thurifers and choristers. These, with some of the better class of artificers, smiled with conscious importance, as specially nominated guests at the feast which the Ramsey monks brought with them for their entertainment in the parish gild-hall. The rest of the crowd, consisting of mariners and farm churls, were curious rather than enthusiastic, and more suspicious than curious: for Ramsey is far from Soham, and ancient adage told them that *fýnd synt feorbúend* — far-dwellers are enemies. At the first landing of the venerable passengers a temporary disturbance was caused by Grim, the fisherman of Ely monastery, who provocatively bit his thumb at the starboard bow oar of the abbat's crew. When this difference had been adjusted by the intervention of the district hundred-man the procession was started for the church. At the tail of it, behind the boat-carls, stalked a blackavised monk of Ely, Peter by name, who pointedly withdrew from an official part in the ceremonies.

The banquet in the gild-hall was altogether a splendid affair. In the whole of their official experience the reeve, the hundred-man, and the local clergy had never received so warm a welcome or participated in such royal cheer. No thin English vintage this that was passed to them in the loving cup, fresh from dignified and consecrated lips, but rich old wine, warmed by Greek suns and cooled in the caverns of Ramsey cellars. The cottars who were admitted at the lower board had never known what it was to have so much ale, and so good, as the monastic vats supplied. Brother Peter of Ely looked on from the door, but took no part in the entertainment. He remarked that the Ramsey dignitaries were modest drinkers, and that the boat-carls looked at their blisters and passed the can to their Soham neighbours with the merest pretence of absorption.

As the liquor in the wassail bowls ebbed a gradual silence crept on the festal party. One after other, official and reverend heads declined upon the board: rustic bodies dropped from their benches on the floor, and stertorous slumber filled the hall. Only the abbat and prior sat erect and looked about them with ferret eyes, and the boat-carls spat on their hands and inspected their blisters. Brother Peter withdrew to the mere-strand, and by the lapping waters mused on the weakness of human heads and the shocking aspect of intemperance in which one has not participated.

What is this spectacle which presents itself to Brother Peter, meditative on the muddy margin of Soham mere, at the grey hour when country cocks do crow and bells do toll? A procession, silent but solid, actual not ghostly, of ten men bearing a coffer strung upon poles. Two dignified figures, their heads wrapt from the raw air in their hoods, bring up the rear. So our friends are making an early and unannounced departure! This is no time to ask the wherefore. Brother Peter tucks up his frock and runs his fleetest to the church. When he looks back from the porch he sees a vessel launched on the shimmering lake, with a broadening track of broken water in its wake.

The abbat and his men are two miles away over the mere when a strange clamour reaches their ears. Horns are blown; a church bell clangs; cries of "Haro" echo over the water; lights flash upon the strand. The boat-carls rest upon their oars; the abbat smiles; the prior chuckles. "Two miles: impossible!" says he; "and, as lay-brother Oswald was so prudent as to hide the oars of the Ely boat in the church tower, they won't get started in a hurry."

The prior sits in the sternage and directs the vessel's course. Between him and the abbat Saint Felix reposes in his box. As they quit the mere and enter the narrow channel which connects it with the Ouse the abbat suggests a psalm and raises *Jubilate Deo*. The bow oars respond with a three-man glee in the fen-men's fashion.

Sleeping Barway they pass, well out of hearing of their pursuers, and then they take the right hand fork of the river, and follow the Ouse stream which we now call the West River. Here they find themselves in a maze of willow-fringed islets and wandering channels which quit and re-enter the main stream. The sopping, gurgling freshets that drain the shallow meres on either hand, as the tidal waters drop, warn them of the perils of a divergence from the river's course. But prior Alfwin knows what he is about, and holds on in the channel that in ten miles will bring them to Erith bank. Nevertheless their transit, impeded by snags and shallows and fallen trees, is of necessity slow. Under such circumstances one must think it an unwarranted security that induced some of the boat-carls to open a spare beer jar and beguile their toil with ill-timed refreshment. Three comatose bodies under the thwarts impose a severe addition of labour on the more self-respecting members of the crew.

It is the hour of prime, and alas! Brother Alfwin, where are we now? Indubitably we are stuck in the mud, and the water is falling. We land on soggy banks, and with labour the boat-carls lift and pole the barge into deeper waters. The operation is repeated several times. Faint cries of "Haro" are borne by the breeze over the fens, and the Lord Abbat shudders with cold and fright. Praised be the saints, at last we are back in the main stream. But what is this? Is not this the identical snag on which we nearly wrecked ourselves the best part of an hour ago? *Deus in adjutorium!* Here is the black prow of the Ely barge rounding the corner, not a hundred yards away, and Monk Peter stands in the bows, raucously shouting and shaking his fist at us! Half-naked figures start up out of the fen and run, hopping from tuft to tuft, on the bank, cheering and waving as they run – friends, foes, or simple spectators, who knows?

The long sweeps of the boat-carls churn the water into oozy froth as they bend themselves with frenzied energy to their task. Foot by foot the Ely men gain upon their predecessors. The game is up unless, as the stroke oars suggest, they lighten ship by heaving Saint Felix into the river. Rather a muddy death than so! Courage! We are less than a mile from Erith.

Lauded be the good Saint Felix, who miraculously interposes for our salvation from the jaws of destruction. Sudden, mysterious, a blanket of white fog rises from the fens and envelopes the river banks. Blotted out are the runners: they cry and wave no more. The Ely prow is swallowed up in vacuous whiteness: the swish of the Ely oars is silenced, and Monk Peter's voice is raised in objurgation. They have run upon that willow that grows aslant the brook, and it is to be doubted that their bows are staved in. Were it not a Christian act to hail them with a loud *Benedicite* in parting? And here is Erith strand and Brother Brihtmer and the Ramsey men. Brother Alfwin, it will be proper for you to give direction to the kitchener for a suitable congratulation for the brethren at supper to-night. To-morrow we will deliberate on the matter of the bell-tower.

"Candid reader," says the Ramsey chronicler, "this is a queer tale. The authority for it is ancient but shaky — *fluctuans veterum nobis tradidit relatio*. I by no means require you to believe it, provided only that in any case you have unhesitating faith that the relics of Saint Felix were translated from the aforesaid town of Soham to Ramsey church, and that there the saint confers inestimable benefits on his worshippers." Ramsey Abbey is gone: the shrine of Saint Felix is gone. The tale of the boat race remains. I ask you to believe it, if you can.

In the Fens

The Sacrist of Saint Radegund

ON A CERTAIN day in mid June in the year 1431 the tolling of the bell in St Radegund's church tower announced to the neighbours of the Priory that a nun was to be buried that day.

In an interval between church services the nuns wander in the garden, which is also the graveyard of St Radegund's, and lies sequestered next the chancel walls. To-day they are drawn thither by a new-made empty grave; for a funeral is a mildly exciting incident in conventual routine. But three sisters sit in the cloister on the stone bench next the chapter door. Also a small novice is curled up on the paved floor with her back against the bench. The day is warm, and the church wall casts a grateful shadow where they sit.

And, because labour and silence are enjoined in the cloister, they rest, and two of them gossip, and Agnes Senclowe, the novice, listens and lays to heart.

The two who gossip are Joan Sudbury, succentrix, and Elizabeth Daveys, who is older than Joan, and holds no office in the monastery. With them sits, and half dozes, Emma Denton, who is very old and very infirm. She does not gossip, for she has hardly spoken a word of sense these forty years past. She is a heavy affliction to the cloister society. She lives mainly in the infirmary, and does not attend church. She knows when it is the hour for a meal, and she knows very little else. If she speaks an intelligible word, it is about something that happened forty years ago. She remembers the great pestilence in 1390.

What ailed poor sister Emma to bring her to this sad pass? When she was young she was something of a religious enthusiast, and because enthusiasm was rare in the cloister, she was promoted by her sisters to high station. When they made her Sacrist she had her one and dearest wish. To have the charge of the beautiful church, of the books, vestments and jewels of the sanctuary, to live in the holy place, with holy thoughts for companions, and in the unfailing round of holy duties – was not that a happy lot? Dignified too the office was; for in the little cloister world the Prioress herself was scarcely a greater lady than the Sacrist. The Sacrist did not sleep with the other nuns in the dormitory; her constant duties did not allow her ordinarily to take her meals in the refectory. Like the Prioress, she had her own servant to attend her, her own house to dwell in. Her habitation was built against the northern chancel wall, and consisted of two chambers. From the upper room, through a hole pierced in the wall, she watched the never-dying light that hung before the High Altar.

But it was not good to be Sacrist for long. The unvarying routine of duty produces torpidity; holy thoughts uncommunicated end in cessation of thought; the solitude was deadly. The office was not coveted by the sisterhood, and was seldom held for more than a year or two together. Wherefore they rejoiced when Emma Denton held it for nine years. For nine years she trimmed the sacred lamp. During nine years her own light dwindled out, and at last the world became dark to sister Emma.

The crazy belfry rocked with the swaying of the bell, which, being cracked, was doubly dolorous. The sound of it roused old sister Emma to a dim consciousness of what was passing, and she spoke to nobody in particular.

"The bell," she said, "the bell again! Last week it tolled, and we buried two. Now there are two more in the dead-house."

"The saints protect us!" said sister Joan; "she is at her old talk of the pestilence year."

"It was Assumption Day," continued the old nun, "when we buried them. We had no Mass that day. To-day it is the cellaress and sister Margery Cailly – God pardon her for a sinful woman. No; Margery is sick, not dead; and I forget, I forget."

"Margery Cailly." cried Joan Sudbury, "what quoth she of Margery Cailly, that goes to her grave to-day? Margery Cailly, that has been our most religious Sacrist ever since yonder poor thing fell beside her wits."

"Religious you may call her," said Elizabeth Daveys, "but God knows, and sister Emma knows, that of her which we know not. Thirty years have I lived in St Radegund's, and I remember not the time when any but Margery was our Sacrist, and well I know that the sacristy has been her prison all those days. But I have heard sister Emma say in her dull way that Margery once knew the convent prison too."

"Well, twelve years I have spent here, and never had speech with the Sacrist. Once I was alone in the church when it was dark, and the daylight only lingered aloft in the roof, and of a sudden I lighted on her in the chancel, busied in her office. Her pale face in her black hood showed like a spirit's, and I thought it was the blessed Radegund that had come down from her window, and I was horribly afraid."

"I think that from the sacristy window her eye followed me about the garden as I walked there," said Elizabeth. "It follows me still, and it makes my flesh creep. What good woman would shun her sisters so? Heaven rest her soul, for be sure she has much to answer for. If she has confessed herself, it is not to our confessor or the Prioress, for I think she has hardly spoken these many years to any but Alice Portress that waits on her."

"Yes, Alice was with her at the end. It was Alice that dug the grave; Alice rings the knell; Alice laid her out in her Sacrist's chamber, and she has placed two white roses on the dead woman's breast."

"Roses?" said Elizabeth Daveys; "roses are not for dead nuns. Whence got she roses?"

"That I can tell you," said the novice, glad to take her part in the conversation, "for Alice told me herself. She got them from the churchyard of St Peter's on the hill."

The office for the dead was said, the empty grave was filled, and Alice the Portress was closeted with the Prioress.

"To you, lady Prioress — not to the Nuns in Chapter — I confess the sin of my youth; not to them, nor yet to you while sister Margery lived. She is gone, and why should I remain? Forty years we shared the secret. She is past censure or forgiveness. On me let the blame rest. I ask no pardon, but only to be dismissed from the house of St Radegund, that I have so unworthily served.

"There is none but myself and poor sister Emma that remembers St Radegund's before the pestilence year. I was but a child then, and my mother was Portress before me. My mother often brought me to the lodge, and I used to play with the novices, or sit at the gate when my mother was away. Margery had but lately come to St Radegund's — seventeen, perhaps, or eighteen years of age she was. Hers was a proud family — the Caillys of Trumpington, and they were rich, and good to St Radegund's. They are gone and forgotten now, but often have I heard old Thomas Key tell of them, for he was a Trumpington man, and he knew the De Freviles of Shelford too. There are De Freviles at Shelford yet, but I think that none there remembers young Nicholas De Frevile that was Sir Robert's son.

"I had a child's thought — that Margery was the most beautiful

Entrance to Chapter House.

creature in the wide world – most beautiful and best. And because she was young and fair and gracious in speech even our hard sisters loved her, and thought it pity of the world when her fair tresses were shorn and she took the ugly veil. For Margery was not religious. God pardon me for my sinful words, but I think she was meant for better things than religion and a cloister. And though she was good and kind to all, Margery did not take to our sisters. There was some trouble – I know not what, for she never told – and for some family reason she was sent to St Radegund's, and ill she liked it. So she went about her work in cloister and church, grieving; and there was talk of her among the sisters. Some thought, some said, that they knew, but Margery said nothing.

"It is all forgotten now, for the pestilence wiped out the memory of those days. Scarcely twelve months had gone since she took the veil when Margery Cailly disappeared from the Priory. You may think what babble of tongues there was in our parlour – how they who were wisest had always known how it would be, and the rest rebuked them for not telling them beforehand. And so for another twelvemonth she was lost to us, and some sisters, who were kind, hoped that she would come back, and some who were kinder, hoped she would not.

"Then, one day in the year before the pestilence, comes an apparitor with our lost Margery, and a letter to the Prioress from the Lord Bishop of Ely. The letter is to say that the Archbishop of Canterbury, in his visitation of Lincoln diocese, has found Margery there, living a secular life; and because secular life is sin to those who have entered the religious order, he commits her to his brother of

Ely, in order that the lost sheep may be restored to the fold where she was professed. And his Lordship of Ely – Heaven help him for a blundering bachelor! – directs that she shall be committed to the convent prison-house until she repents of her wickedness, and when she is loosed from it, shall make public confession in Chapter, and implore the pardon of the sisters for her enormities.

"Our Prioress was kinder to Margery than the Bishop meant – who could not be kind to her? Her prison life was no longer than would satisfy the Bishop's enquiries, and as for the confession in the Chapter-house – it never happened. There were some, though they liked not confession for themselves, who thought an opportunity was missed, and blamed the Prioress; for cloister talk is dull if we know not one another's failings. Still, the sisters were kind to Margery, and very kind when they wanted to get the secret from her. But she said never a word about it, unless it were to the Prioress. Beautiful she was as ever, but grief and humiliation were on her, heavy as death, and because she confided in none, she lost the friendship of the sisters. To me, who was but a child, she would talk, but scarcely to another, and her talk with me was never about herself.

"One other there was with whom sometimes she had speech, and that was old Thomas Key, maltster and trusty servant in general matters of the Priory. Him she had known in happier days when he was a tenant of the Caillys at Trumpington. Her family was too proud and too pious to remember the disgraced nun, and they never visited her; but from Thomas she learnt something of home and the outside world.

"Then came the dreadful year when the pestilence raged in Cambridge town. The nuns had been used to get leave from the Prioress to go out into the town, but there was no gadding now. The gate was closely barred, and none were admitted from outside except Thomas Key. We carried the Host in procession about the Nuns' Croft and – laud be to the saints! – it protected our precincts from the contagion. And while the sinful world without died like the beasts that perish, we sat secure, but frightened, in our cloister, and blessed our glorious saint for extending the protection of her prayers over the pious few who did her service in St Radegund's.

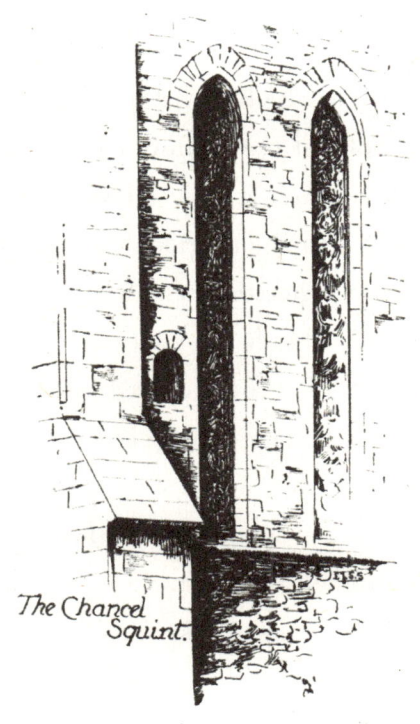

The Chancel Squint.

"You have heard how the parish clergy died that year. One, two, sometimes three died in one parish, and the Bishop found it hard to provide successors. Boys that had barely taken the tonsure a week before were sent in haste to anoint the sick and bury the dead in places where the plague had left an unshepherded flock. Sir John Dekyn, priest of St Peter's church on the hill, was one that died, and his successor did not live a fortnight after him. Then we heard from Thomas Key that a mere youth had taken the place, one Sir Nicholas of the Shelford De Frevile family, who had but lately been ordered priest at Ely. And we were told that he worked with a feverous zeal among the poor, the sick, and the dying of his parish.

"Now when this news was brought to sister Margery by Thomas Key, it was to her as a summons from death to life. Her eye brightened and her cheek glowed when she heard of the heroic goodness of this young priest. While the sisters shuddered and shrank at each morning's fatal news, she was consumed with a passionate desire to know what was passing in the plague-stricken town, and she plied my mother and Thomas Key with incessant questionings. 'Who was sick of the townsfolk? Were any of the clergy visited? How went it with the poor in St Peter's, where the pestilence was hottest?' For some weeks she heard that the light burned still at night in St Peter's parsonage, and that the priest was unscathed, incessant in his ministrations and blessed by his parishioners. And it seemed as though the sickness was abating.

"Then, late one afternoon in early August, there came a call for Margery. Thomas Key brought it, and whether it was his own tidings or a message from some other, I cannot say; Margery never told me. But this I know, that she took me apart in the cloister and spoke to me, and she was terribly moved and her voice was choked. 'Little Alice,' she said, 'as you love me, get me the gate-key after Lauds tonight. It is life or death to me to go out into the town. Only do it, and say nothing — no, not to your mother.' Young as I was, I knew how the nuns were used to humour my mother into letting them pass the gate; but that was in day-time. At night, in our besieged state, with the death-bells tolling all around, it seemed a terrible thing to venture. But I asked no questions. Say it was the recklessness of a girl — say it was the love that I bore to Margery. I stole the key and gave it to her after sundown.

"What happened afterwards I will tell you as it was told to me by Thomas Key, who waited for her outside the gate. They passed along the dark, deserted streets. The plague-fires burnt low in the middle of the roadway, but there were none to tend them, and no living thing they saw but the starving dogs, herded at barred doors. They crossed the bridge and mounted to St Peter's church. The priest's manse — you know it — is a low house next the church. A white rose, still in flower, clambered on its walls, and, half hidden by its sprays, a taper gleamed through the open window; but there was no sound of life within. They pushed open the door and entered.

"Stretched on his pallet, forsaken and untended, lay the young priest of St Peter's, the pangs of death upon him. Margery threw herself on her knees by his bed-side, and Thomas watched and waited. For a time there was silence, for Margery had no voice to pray. Only at times the dying man grumbled and wandered in his talk; but little he said that Thomas understood.

"Then after a long time, he stirred himself uneasily and uttered one word, 'Margery.' And she — alas the day! — put out her arm and laid it on his shoulder. In an instant the dying man half raised himself on his bed and turned his eyes on her, and there was recognition in them. And one arm he threw about her neck, and felt blindly for the fair locks that had been shorn long since, and he said heavily and painfully, 'Margery, *belle amie*, let us go to the pool above the mill, where the great pike lie, and sun and shadow lie on the deep water.' So Thomas knew that they were boy and girl again by the old mill at Trumpington.

"That was all, and the end came soon. They two laid him decently beneath his white sheet, and Margery plucked two white roses from the spray that straggled across his window, and laid them on the dead man's breast. So they left him, with the candle still burning out into the dark.

"There was a horrible dread in St Radegund's when, four days later, sister Margery sickened of the pestilence; and it was worse when we learnt soon after that Thomas Key was visited – then that he was dead. That was the beginning of our sorrows. You have heard, Lady Prioress, how three sisters died before August was out, how most of the others deserted the house, and some never returned to it. Our prayers were unheard, and to us who remained it seemed as if the saints slept, or God were dead.

"So it happened that when the plague abated, and the first meeting was held in St Radegund's Chapter-house, about St Luke's day in the autumn, there were only three to attend it – the Prioress, the Sacrist (Emma Denton), and Margery Cailly. For – wonderful it seems – Margery, who least needed to live, was the one spared of those who were taken with the pestilence. Presently some old sisters returned, and new ones took the place of the departed. But the sword of the pestilence cut off the memory of the old days, and the sins and sufferings, the virtues and the victories of the former sisterhood were a forgotten dream when the cloister filled again. So when Emma Denton passed into her lethargy, and Margery Cailly earnestly petitioned to fill her place in the Sacristy, there was not a sister to question her character and devoutness.

"Not yesterday, but forty years ago, Margery Cailly passed out of life; for you know that, save to me, she had spoken few words since. And though I have waited on her for most of those years she never breathed to me the name of Nicholas De Frevile, never hinted at the story of her unhappy girlhood. But once in the springtime, just after she entered her Sacrist prison-house, she entreated me to plant a white rose-bush on the grave of the young priest of St Peter's. I did so, and have renewed it since, and one day, by your grace, I shall plant a spray of the same roses where she lies apart from him. I have confessed my wrong in stealing the key and bringing death into the cloister. If you can forgive me, so; if not, all I ask is that you let your sinful servant depart in peace."

There is a curious aperture in the outer northern wall of the chancel of the nuns' church which is now Jesus College Chapel. If it is examined its purpose is evident. It was the lychnoscope, through which the Sacrist watched by night the light before the High Altar. It is the sole abiding memorial of Margery Cailly, Sacrist of St Radegund.